"His character a nice, low-key of-place are ge lence are almost _____ told with distaste for the _____ of human flesh . . . But above all he was—and still is—readable, in the best sense of that term."

—Bill Pronzini, *Mystery Scene*

"Bob Martin was a very popular writer in his day . . . Quality-wise, I would say he wrote as well as early Ross Macdonald and John D. MacDonald . . . His most successful novel appears to have been *Little Sister* [which] went through six U.S. printings."

—Jim Felton, *Mystery*File*

Little Sister

by Robert Martin
Writing as Lee Roberts

Black Gat Books • Eureka California

LITTLE SISTER

Published by Black Gat Books
A division of Stark House Press
1315 H Street
Eureka, CA 95501, USA
griffinskye3@sbcglobal.net
www.starkhousepress.com

ISBN-13: 978-1-951473-07-5

Book design by Jeff Vorzimmer, *¡caliente!design*, Austin, Texas
Proofreading by Bill Kelly
Cover art by Rudy Nappi, originally from *Reefer Girl* by Jane
Manning.

First Stark House Press/Black Gat Edition: August 2020

Robert Martin
by Bill Pronzini

As with any large group, professional writers come in all sizes, shapes, races, creeds, colors, attitudes, dispositions, and personalities. Some are eccentrics, like Jay Flynn. Some are breast-beaters, literary narcissists. Some are just plain fundaments (to use the polite term). Most are pretty good folks, generally. And a few—a very few—are intrinsically, unassumingly nice people: the kind, if you could pick and choose, you might want as a close friend, a spouse, a parent or grandparent.

Robert Lee Martin was one of that last, small category. A genuinely nice man who deserved a hell of a lot better than he got out of this life.

You can't always tell from reading a writer's fiction what sort of person he or she is, but in some instances you can be fairly sure. I was sure about Bob long before I had any personal contact with him. All of his fictional series heroes—private eyes Jim Bennett and Lee Fiske, and Doctor Clinton Shannon (nee Clinton Colby in early pulp stories)—aren't just good guys, they're nice guys. Problems, yes. Quirks and foibles, yes. Lapses in taste and judgment and morality, yes. They wouldn't be real and you wouldn't care what happens to them, otherwise. But underneath, at the core of their humanity—nice guys, by God.

A Midwesterner, born in 1910, Bob lived most of his life in the Cleveland area. He was a personnel manager by profession, with an industrial manufacturing company, and did pretty well at it—well enough to support a wife and three children in relative comfort. He was an avid reader (Chandler, Hammett, James M. Cain, Hemingway, Steinbeck, Maugham, Fitzgerald), and in the late thirties he decided to try his hand at stories for the pulp magazines. It wasn't long before he

was selling steadily to Popular Publications: through-
out the forties and into the early fifties his name was
cover-featured on *Dime Detective*, where the bulk of
his stories appeared, as well as on such other magazines as *Black Mask, Detective Tales, New Detective,
All-Story Detective*, and *15-Story Detective*. An occasional Popular reject appeared in *Thrilling Detective*
and *Mammoth Detective*, among others.

Most of his *Dime Detective* novelettes and novellas
feature Jim Bennett, head of the Cleveland office of the
New York-based American (later American-Interna-
tional) Detective Agency. In one sense the Bennett stories are typical pulp fare, in that they contain plenty of
rough-and-tumble action; but in another sense they're
unusual because they also place strong emphasis on de-
tection and character, particularly that of Bennett himself. In an era when first-person private eyes were often
little more than boozing, wenching, wise-cracking ci-
phers, Bennett comes off as a real and intelligent human being: a man tough when he has to be, yet gentle,
likable, and vulnerable. The same is true of Lee Fiske
and Clinton Colby/Shannon, though to a somewhat
lesser degree: neither is as sharply delineated as Bennett.

A few other protagonists made a pulp appearance
now and then—a PI named Deegan, an insurance dick
called Regent—but for the most part Bob left his fictional detecting up to Bennett, Fiske and Doctor Clint.
He also preferred rural and small-town settings to an
urban one: many more of his stories are laid in villages,
on farms and ranches in the vicinity of Cleveland and
other parts of northern Ohio than in Cleveland itself.

When the pulp markets began to decline in the early
fifties, Bob turned to novels. And like Chandler and
numerous others, yours truly included, he also turned
to the cannibalizing of his own short stories—almost
exclusively, those published in *Dime Detective*—for

the plots of those novels, with varying degrees of success.

His first book, *Dark Dream* (Dodd, Mead, 1951) is an interesting but flawed blend of two Jim Bennett novelettes: "Death Under Par" (Dime Detective, May 1947) and "Death Gives a Permanent Wave" (*DD*, October 1947). *The Little Sister* (Gold Medal, 1952)— the first of seven titles to appear under Bob's pseudonym of Lee Roberts—features Lee Fiske and is an effective expansion of "Pardon My Poison" (*DD*, April 1948). The second Bennett, *Sleep, My Love* (Dodd, 1953), is another and better fusion of two novelettes: "Case of the Careless Caress" (*DD*, January 1948), which features Lee Fiske rather than Bennett, and "I'll Be Killing You" (*DD*, February 1950).

Several other Bennett novels also have their origins in the pulps, including three of the best in the series: *Tears for the Bride* (Dodd, 1954), in which Bennett becomes enmeshed in a shooting and other intrigue on a cattle ranch owned by the parents of his secretary and love interest, Sandy Hollis ("Killers Can't Be Careless," *DD*, November 1946); *To Have and To Kill* (Dodd, 1960), about murder among a wedding party on a fancy Lake Erie estate ("A Shroud for Her Trousseau," *DD*, June 1949); and *A Coffin for Two* (Hale, 1964), about odd doings connected with a family burial vault in a small town ("Death Under Glass," *DD*, February 1952. another Lee Fiske vehicle).

Between 1951 and 1960, Bob published ten Bennett novels with Dodd, Mead (two of which were the bases for episodes of the TV series *77 Sunset Strip* and *Surfside Six*); a second Fiske, as by Roberts, also with Dodd: two Clinton Shannons, one Dodd and one Gold Medal; and three nonseries suspense novels, two as by Roberts and all with Dodd.

The best of the non-series books, and one of his best overall, is *Judas Journey* (1956), as by Roberts.

It's atypical of Bob's work for three reasons: first; because the setting is Texas and Mexico; second, because the protagonist, oilfield worker Rackwell Ramsey, is not a nice guy, is in fact something of a heel almost to the very end; and third, because it contains a surprising amount—by the standards of the hardcover mystery in 1956—of fairly steamy sex. In all of Jim Bennett's cases, he never once gets laid, not even by Sandy Hollis!

Bob was an uneven writer, as so many of us are. Some of his plots work nicely; others clunk along with uneven pacing and not much cohesion. On the plus side: His characters are all believable people; he had a nice, low-key style; his descriptions and sense-of-place are generally excellent; his scenes of violence are almost always understated and told with distaste for the mangling of human flesh. On the debit side: He sometimes had his heroes and other characters act with motivation that is weak and illogical; his dialogue, while usually good, now and then fails to ring true (and in a couple of instances is downright bad); and he had a habit of not tying off some rather large loose ends. But above all he was—and still is—readable, in the best sense of that term. He was never guilty of what John D. MacDonald once referred to as the "Look-Ma-I'm-Writing!" syndrome.

If the fifties was a highly successful decade for Bob, the sixties was the exact opposite—a hideous decade in all respects. The company for which he worked was gobbled up by International Telephone and Telegraph, and Bob eventually resigned when he found that he couldn't function under the conglomerate yoke. His wife fell ill—a long, painful, and financially draining illness that culminated in her death in June of 1970. And for reasons that had to do with declining sales and a changing market for mystery novels, neither Dodd, Mead nor any other American publisher wanted Bob's work between 1961 and 1971. His last four published novels—three Bennetts: *A Coffin for Two, She, Me and Murder*, and *Bargain for Death*; and one Clinton Shannon, *Suspicion*, as by Lee Roberts—found homes only in England in the early sixties and were not brought out here until the short-lived paperback house, Curtis Books, did them in 1971 and 1972.

Bob more or less quit writing in 1963, as a result of all the personal and professional disasters. When I began corresponding with him in 1972, he was working on his first novel in nearly ten years. He lived alone then, in an apartment in Tiffin, Ohio, and relied for his livelihood on a small pension, some scattered royalties and foreign rights checks, and the help of his family.

I initiated the contact between us. In those days I corresponded with a number of writers whose work I had admired over the years: Evan Hunter, Jim McKimmey, Talmage Powell, others. I was living in West Germany, and the more mail from home, the less far-away-from-it-all I felt. I had read Bob's pulp stories in the sixties, when I first began collecting pulps, and enjoyed them, but what made me determined to write to him was a copy of the Curtis Books edition of *Bargain for Death* that I found while on a business trip to New York that spring.

The executive secretary of MWA gave me an address for Bob, which turned out to be twenty years old; why that one was given to me remains a mystery, since he was still a member of MWA and had provided the organization with his current address. But by a lucky coincidence, someone in the Tiffin post office knew Bob and was able to route my letter to him.

His response was immediate. He was flattered, he said, to hear from a fellow mystery writer who remembered and admired his work. He'd had precious little contact with writers since his Dodd, Mead days, with two exceptions. One was a fellow pulpster, Cyril Plunkett, who had lived and recently died in Toledo. The other was John D. MacDonald, whom he had known ever since they shared an agent—Joseph T. "Cap" Shaw, of *Black Mask* fame—during their pulp-writing days in the late forties. Bob spoke highly of John D., both as a writer and a person.

In a 1975 letter, Bob wrote that he had been "smack in the middle" of a hassle between John and newspaper columnist and bestselling writer Jim Bishop the previous year. It seems Bishop implied in a column that he had "discovered" John when he, Bishop, was an editor at Fawcett Gold Medal in 1949, by persuading the late Bill Engle to publish *The Brass Cupcake*. Bob sent the column to MacDonald, whose reply was that Bishop "must have fallen out of his tree or something" and had "disinterred Bill, skinned him and was wearing his skin," for Bishop had had nothing to do with the purchase of *The Brass Cupcake*.

Bob received permission to send John's letter to Bishop, who wrote back giving names, dates and other pertinent facts about his editorial duties at Gold Medal (which MacDonald again disputed) and in the bargain indulged in the most arrogant sort of literary snobbism: "There is no credit in 'discovering' a John Mac-Donald. His books are successful and make money, but I would prefer to have discovered a Thomas Wolfe or even an Irwin Shaw..."

Bob and I exchanged several letters in 1972. I was then working on the third "Nameless" novel, *Undercurrent*, and I wrote him of my intention to dedicate the book to him, John D., and several other writers whose pulp fiction I particularly enjoyed. (Which in fact I did.) His response was typical of the man: "I am honored and flattered that you have included me in the dedication of the Random House novel. It is one of the nicest things that ever happened to me, and the very first time I have been mentioned in a book dedication... I am sending a copy [of your letter] to my agent, who will be as pleased as I am. I certainly do want a copy of the book—but autographed—when it comes out."

We fell out of touch before *Undercurrent* was published (although I eventually did see to it that he received an inscribed copy). It was my fault; I had decided to move back to this country in 1973 and was so busy making preparations and trying to finish a couple of novel projects that I let more than one correspondence lapse. As a result it was more than two years before Bob and I began to regularly exchange letters again.

He reestablished contact in September of 1975. And his four-page letter was not a happy one. From the fall of '74 to the spring of '75 he had been seriously ill and partially disabled with a spinal arthritic condition. Since recovering, he had spent some pleasant days in Texas with his son and the son's family, and with his brother, a doctor and former coroner who lived on Lake Erie, but for the most part, he said, "There are so few people I see or talk to. My children have their own lives and families, which is as it should be, but I am lonely much of the time."

His attempt at a career comeback had been unsuccessful. The novel he had been writing in 1972, a non-series mystery called *A Time of Evil*, had not sold; neither had a Jim Bennett, *A Friend of the Family*, he'd written the previous year. An editor at Pinnacle had jerked him around on *Friend* for months, promising to buy it as soon as he could find a slot, only to eventually return the manuscript with the excuse that he was still over-inventoried—a bitter disappointment to Bob. He lamented to me that he had begun to wonder if he had been out of touch with the markets for too long, or if perhaps the problem was his agent, who had been swallowed up by a large, high-powered outfit that specialized in film deals as well as book sales. He was "beginning to have the feeling that I am in another ITT situation ... a tiny frog in a mighty big puddle."

He asked if I could recommend a small agent who might be willing to work with him. "I am good for at least two or three mystery and detective novels a year," he wrote, "60,000 to 80,000 words each... Writing is not just a hobby with me; after I left ITT I counted on writing income to supplement my small pension benefits. And I truly feel that the last two books are as good as any I've written."

I gave Bob a name—not a good one, dammit, though at the time I thought this agent was among the best—and he wrote the person asking for representation. He was turned down. But he remained as optimistic as always; he had a burning desire to get back into print and believed that sooner or later be would sell a new book. I believed it too. Early in 1976 I offered to read the two unpublished manuscripts, to maybe offer some marketing advice.

I don't know if Bob would have taken me up on my offer. I don't know if his manuscripts might have sold with the right agent handling them; I only know that they didn't sell and now never will.

Bob Martin died before he could answer my letter.

When I didn't hear from him within a few weeks—he was almost always prompt with his replies, even if I wasn't with mine—I began to worry that something was wrong. I was about to write again when I received a letter from his son in Texas, with the news that Bob had passed away. The son was letting me know because Bob had spoken fondly of me, and because he (the son) had found my last letter among Bob's papers.

I never met Bob Martin face to face; I have never even seen a photograph of him. And yet, the news of his death moved me close to tears. To this day I'm not quite sure why. A combination of things, I guess: the fact that he was a nice man, a man I wish I had met and known better and perhaps helped in some small meaningful way; the fact that he had so much tragedy and adversity in his life; the fact that those last two novels of his never sold, and would never sell, and he wanted so desperately to be a published writer again.

And those two haunting sentences in his 1975 letter: "There are so few people I see or talk to. My children have their own lives and families, which is as it should be, but I am lonely much of the time."

To close that same '75 letter, he wrote: "One of the few Spanish phrases I know is, 'Adios, amigo,' which I thought meant simply, 'Goodbye, friend,' but in Texas I learned that the true translation is 'Go with God, my friend.' And so ... adios, amigo."

Adios, amigo, I thought that day in 1976. At least you're not lonely anymore.

[This article first appeared in *Mystery Scene* #14. Copyright © 1988 by Bill Pronzini.]

Little Sister

by Robert Martin

Writing as Lee Roberts

Chapter One

A fat little maid told me Miss Prosper was expecting me and that I would find her on the rear lawn. I thanked her, walked down the steps to the wide front porch, and moved across freshly cut grass until I came to a flagstone walk. I followed the walk past a cement drive, a big three-car garage, a swimming pool, and a huge rose trellis, and emerged upon three acres of lawn slanting down to the lake. The sun was shining and the lake was a glimmering blue. White-tipped breakers lapped lazily at the edge of the narrow beach.

It wasn't difficult to locate Vivian Prosper. The rug-sized towel upon which she was lying made a white island on the smooth expanse of green. She had a long golden-brown body and her face was upturned to the morning sun. Her arms were flung wide, her honey-colored hair fanned out on the towel beneath her head, and one slim leg was bent a little, very gracefully. Green-tinted sunglasses shielded her eyes. She was wearing a scanty pair of white shorts that I could easily have wadded into a vest pocket, and green sandals. And that was all. A thin white sweater lay beside her.

I stood still for maybe a minute trying to decide what to do. Finally I turned and tiptoed back beyond the rose trellis. Then I retraced my steps down the walk, clicking my heels briskly. As I stepped to the lawn once more I saw that she was sitting up with her back toward me, slowly pulling the white sweater down over her head. She gazed at me over one rounded shoulder. I moved across the grass until I stood at the edge of the big towel. The white sweater fitted her very snugly.

She removed the sunglasses and flung her hair back from her face with a graceful motion of her head. At close range I saw that she was between twenty-five and thirty. She had a full red mouth, a thin straight nose, and eyes that matched the blue-green of Lake Erie on a sunny day.

She said coolly, "I heard you the first time."

"Sorry," I said. "What was I supposed to do? Yell, 'One, two, three, here I come, ready or not'?"

She didn't smile. "You're Brice?" Her tone indicated that I could have been the new butler reporting for duty.

I nodded.

Her gaze went over me slowly. "You don't look like a detective."

"Want to see my bullet scars?"

She frowned slightly with a faint expression of distaste, got lazily to her feet, and picked up the towel. "Come inside," she said shortly.

I followed her up the walk past the rose trellis, the swimming pool, the big garage. It was a pleasure to see her move. We entered a side door of the house, moved down a cool dusky hall until we came to a living room only a little smaller than a basketball court. A wide expanse of window overlooked the lake. There was a deep green rug, a long tomato-red divan, a big porcelain fireplace, a few heavy deep chairs and some spindly ones, a low glass coffee table. She motioned me carelessly to one of the chairs and crossed to a small mahogany desk in a corner. I remained standing.

Over her shoulder she asked, "How much do you charge?"

"For what?"

She turned impatiently, annoyance in her blue-green eyes. "For your services. What is your fee? I want to write you a check."

"Miss Prosper," I said gently, "you called my office and said you had some work you wanted done. You asked for Andrew H. Brice personally, and I was flattered. Nevertheless, I did some routine checking. I

found that your stepfather is the well-known sports-
man Jerome K. Pitt. I also learned that you recently
divorced your husband, Allan Frederick Keeler, to
whom you had been married for almost two years.
You divorced him on the grounds of mental cruelty,
whatever the hell that is, and since there were no children, you reverted to your maiden name of Vivian
Prosper and continued to live with your sister, Linda,
and your stepfather."

I paused and then added, "Do you want to hear
more?"

"By all means." There was a faint glint of amuse-
ment in her eyes.

"All right. Your sister is seventeen years old; she is
much too pretty for her own good and she has a police
record for drunken driving. Your ex-husband is a
pharmacist, and at present he is employed by the Apex
Drug Company in their big store on the east side of
this city. Your father, Abner Quentin Prosper, made a
pile of money in the trucking business. He died six
years ago, leaving everything to your mother, who was
later remarried to Jerome K. Pitt. Three years ago your
mother died, leaving a big chunk of her estate in trust
funds for you and your sister, and the balance to Jerome. I don't know what you want of me, but I'm here
to find out, and after I find out I'll tell you whether or
not I'll take the job and how much it will cost you." I
took a deep breath. It had been a long speech for me.

For the first time she smiled. "I'll say this, Mr.
Brice: You are thorough."

I nodded and tried to keep from staring at her.

She took a cigarette from a silver box on the glass
table, flicked flame from a matching silver lighter, and
exhaled smoke at the ceiling. "It's Linda, of course,"
she said. "My kid sister. Mother left some money in
trust for her, as you said, and she gets it next month,
on her eighteenth birthday. After Mother died I tried
to look after Linda, but I'm afraid I haven't done a very

good job. Now she tells me that she's going to marry a man named Arthur Spotwood. I want you to break up the affair. I don't care how."

"How much will she get?"

"Close to three hundred thousand dollars."

I tried to visualize that much money. I couldn't, and I said, "I see. And you think this Spotwood wants to marry her for the money?"

She nodded. "I'm sure of it."

"All right. What else is wrong with him?"

She waved her cigarette impatiently. "Everything. He's much older than Linda, he's been married before, and he runs a gasoline station. He's just not our—her type."

"Does your sister love him?"

She moved her shoulders beneath the thin sweater. "She's too young to know about love," she said, and she added with a faint trace of bitterness, "whatever love is. Arthur Spotwood is rather handsome, and he's older. Infatuation is a better word."

"How much older?"

"He's about thirty."

"That's not exactly June and January," I said. "Have you talked to your sister about him?"

"Several times. She resented it very much."

"What about Spotwood? Have you approached him?"

She looked annoyed. "Of course," she said shortly. "I've tried everything. That's why I called you. I offered Arthur five thousand dollars to leave Linda alone. He refused."

"There's quite a difference between five thousand dollars and three hundred thousand," I said.

"That's obvious," she said coldly.

"Where is your sister now?"

She crushed out her cigarette and averted her eyes. "I don't know. She left here in her car before dinner last night, and she hasn't returned."

I glanced at my wrist watch. Twenty minutes before ten in the morning. "Does she have any other boy friends?"

"Yes, several. But she sees Spotwood more frequently than the others."

"Do you think she's with Spotwood now?"

Again she lifted her round firm shoulders in a careless shrug. "Probably," she said. "I don't know."

I caught myself gazing once more at the white sweater. "What about your stepfather?" I asked. "Can't he help?"

"Jerome?" she said scornfully. "He has more important things to do than to worry about a wayward stepdaughter. Things like golf, and hand-tooled shotguns, and fishing in Canada, and grouse-shooting in Idaho." She gazed at me with level eyes. "Are you going to help me?"

"I'm thinking about it," I said, and I moved to the window.

A red Ford convertible with the top up moved slowly along the drive and drifted to a stop before the big garage. Then its horn began to blow. Nobody got out of the car. It just sat there with the horn blowing. I turned to Vivian Prosper. She was listening intently.

I said, "Does your sister drive a red Ford convertible?"

She nodded silently.

I moved swiftly across the big room and out the door. Vivian Prosper followed me down the dark hall and out to the drive beside the house. The car's horn continued to shatter the morning with a steady blare. I moved to the driver's side.

A girl was slumped forward in the seat with her cheek against the horn ring on the wheel. She had a small, pretty face and a mass of dark brown hair. The hair was tangled and dusty-looking, and there were black smudges on her white linen jacket. Her small hands lay limply at her side and she was breathing heavily.

I opened the door, grasped her by the shoulders, and gently pushed her back against the seat. The horn stopped blowing and the morning was abruptly quiet. The girl's head wobbled sideways and she began to mumble incoherently. There was a strong smell of whisky. I glanced at Vivian Prosper. Her face held a stony expression. I let go of the girl and she started to fall forward. I lowered her to the seat, left her there, and moved around the car. I didn't see any signs of an accident, and I started back toward the front. A brown smear on the polished chrome of the rear bumper stopped me. I tried the handle of the trunk compartment. It was not locked and I lifted the door upward.

Inside, beside the spare tire and wheel, a man was huddled on the black rubber matting. There was congealed blood in the grooves of the matting. The man's face was toward me and his eyes were open. The front of his shirt was a solid sticky mass of blood.

Chapter Two

Vivian Prosper's sandals clicked on the cement as she moved to join me at the rear of the car. She stood beside me and I let her look at what was inside. She looked long and steadily. Then she began to sway a little. I held out an arm to catch her, but she didn't fall.

"W-who is it?" she whispered.

I was surprised. "Don't you know?"

She shook her head slowly. Her eyes were dull with shock, and she was fighting for control.

I touched her arm. "Go ahead—scream."

She flung off my hand with an impatient gesture, and she took a deep breath. "I never scream," she said sharply. "We've got to get Linda in the house."

She moved swiftly to the front of the convertible. I closed the trunk compartment, moved up behind her, pushed her aside, and lifted her sister from the front seat. Her body was light and limp in my arms. I was glad that a high stone wall and a line of shrubbery hid us from the possible prying eyes of neighbors. With Vivian Prosper at my heels I carried the small form of the girl into the house. The fat little maid appeared from somewhere and met us in the hall. She stopped, looked worried, and began to twist her hands together.

Vivian Prosper snapped, "You've seen this before. Get her bed ready."

The maid nodded quickly and ran up the wide stairway. I followed, Vivian Prosper at my side. From a bright sunny hall above we entered a gaily furnished bedroom. The maid had folded back a blue silk cover from a bed and she now fluttered nervously about the room. I laid Linda Prosper on the bed. Her eyes were closed and there were tiny beads of perspiration on her forehead. Curly brown hair clung damply to her cheeks. She had long dark lashes, a small oval face, a short nose, and a plump little mouth. Her older sister had told me that she was seventeen, almost eighteen, but she looked much younger. Her white linen skirt was wrinkled and spotted and twisted up above her knees, exposing a smooth expanse of ivory-white skin above the tops of sand-colored nylons. Her legs were straight and neat, with delicately rounded calves, like a dancer's. On her feet were stubby high-heeled brown-and-white shoes. They were dusty and scuffed.

At a sharp command from Vivian Prosper, the maid hurried out of the room. From down the hall I heard the sound of running water. Vivian brushed me aside, pulled down her sister's skirt, and began to remove the small dusty shoes. "I've got to sober her up," she said curtly, "and find out what happened. I'll take care of her—I'm used to it." She looked up at me. "You'll find liquor in the library."

I didn't move.

She said impatiently, "Don't tell me that a private detective is refusing a drink?"

"Hell, no," I said. "Not me. But there's a dead man in your sister's car. Remember? I'll have to call the police."

She said quietly, "Of course you do. But wait until I come down, will you? Please?"

A shaft of morning sunlight glinted on her tawny hair and caressed her slender figure. There was a sudden softness about her mouth and a desperate pleading look in her eyes. It had been a long time since I'd met a creature as gorgeous as Vivian Prosper. But somehow she was more than simply a super-attractive woman, more attractive and pulse-stirring than any I'd met in all the lonely years I'd worked for one agency or another in cities from New York to Reno to Frisco. Especially Reno. Now at last I was working for myself here in this city on the shore of blue Lake Erie. In all my long years of chasing people on the wrong side of the law, of delving into a thousand worries and secret vices, of meeting the virtuous and the dissolute, the weak and the strong, millionaires and paupers, I'd never met a girl like Vivian Prosper, not another with her looks and her money, and a special something I couldn't explain.

I smiled at her. "Sure, I'll wait for you."

She smiled too, and I think she knew how I felt about her. There was a warmth, a promise, a something in her eyes. "Thank you," she said, and once more she bent over the bed.

I went out quietly and down the stairs. But I didn't go to the library. I went outside, to the red convertible, and I took a quick look around to make certain that the coast was clear. Then once more I lifted the door of the trunk compartment.

The dead man was young, maybe twenty-two or -three, with black hair, trimmed short in a crew cut. A thin white healed scar ran across the bridge of his nose. His eyes were blue, with a dull film over them, and death had made the pupils just a little off center. The wound in his chest had been made by a knife or other sharp instrument. He was wearing a white shirt, open at the neck, a gray tweed coat, gray flannel slacks, and soiled white buckskin shoes with heavy crepe soles. I didn't see a hat. I went through his pockets. I didn't find a thing—no money, no cigarettes, no keys, nothing. Not even an old envelope. There were tobacco crumbs in the left pocket of his jacket where cigarettes had once been, and two broken toothpicks in the other pocket. He wasn't rigid yet, but the muscles were stiffening fast, and if he wasn't moved soon some undertaker was going to have a tough time getting him out of there. I went over him once more, swiftly, avoiding the sticky shirt front. Even the labels in his clothes had been ripped out. I guessed that he'd been dead at least six or eight hours.

I closed the trunk compartment and moved to the front of the convertible. In the dash recess I found an Ohio-Kentucky road map, a half-empty package of cigarettes, and a flashlight that didn't work. I leaned down and peered under the front seat. Something glittered and I reached in and pulled out a silver-colored match folder. Red embossed printing on the cover read: "The Venice Café, 2239 McKinney Road. Dinners, Dancing, Wine, Beer, Mixed Drinks. Guido Santos, Prop."

I pushed the folder back under the seat for the cops to find. Then I went back into the house. It was quiet in the lower hall, but from upstairs I heard the murmur of voices—Vivian Prosper's and the maid's. The library was beyond the alcove off the big living room. I found the liquor supply without any trouble. A fancy built-in bar with an ice unit contained everything from Scotch and bourbon to vermouth and bitters.

I was working on my second modest drink of
Scotch when Vivian Prosper came in. She had replaced
the scanty shorts with tailored fawn-tinted slacks, but
she was still wearing the white sweater. Her yellow
hair fell softly over her shoulders and she looked like
nine million dollars.

"Hello," she said wearily.

I raised my glass. "Hi." I was suddenly happy. She
was something really special to look at and to remember.

She nodded at my glass. "Could I have some of
that?"

"Scotch?"

"Anything."

I made her a drink of Scotch and handed it to her.

She took a slow sip, her eyes thoughtful and re-
mote. Then she moved to the window and stood staring out. In a low tight voice she said, "Are you going
to—to help me?"

"Maybe."

"I really need you now."

I stepped up behind her and stood close. Not too
close, but close enough to smell the faint perfume of
her. From somewhere in the house a clock chimed ten
times. I stirred restlessly and gazed at her yellow hair,
her straight back, and her slim waist. All I could see of
her face was the tip of her nose, one corner of her red
mouth, and the soft curve of a cheek.

I said, "Did your sister tell you anything?"

She spoke without turning. "She's too drunk," she
said bitterly. "I couldn't get anything out of her. She
just mumbled. Once I thought she said, 'Pooh on your
flint points', or something like that. That's what it
sounded like. She's sleeping now. Perhaps she'll tell me
something later." She turned slowly to face me and her
eyes searched mine. "You know what we must do
now?" she said softly.

"Sure. Call the police."

She shook her head. "No, not yet." She paused, watching me, her lips parted a little.

"No?" I raised my eyebrows.

"We've got to get rid of *that*," she said breathlessly. "In her car."

A cold finger seemed to trace my spine. I took a swallow of the whisky before I answered. Then I said carefully, "Thanks just the same, but my fee doesn't include helping to get rid of a dead man."

Her lips curved in a half-smile. When it came to looks she had everything, and a lot more. Lots and lots more. I decided that her ex-husband, Allan Frederick Keeler, had been a dope to let her get away from him. Suddenly I felt contempt for Keeler, and something else. Jealousy?

She held out her empty glass. "More."

Her fingers touched mine as I took the glass. I could see the blue-green lights in her eyes and the faint dusting of freckles over her nose. I guessed that the top of her honey-colored head would fit just beneath my chin. I turned away with a sigh, made her another drink, and reinforced my own a little.

As she took the glass, she said, "You know something?"

"What?"

"I think I like you."

That made us even. I liked her, too. A hell of a lot. Too much, too quick. But there it was. I liked everything about her. A man could search all his life and never find a more desirable chunk of female. And she was rich. Rich and wonderful—with a juvenile delinquent for a sister, who was now upstairs sleeping off a binge, a gay night. A gay night that had ended in the sunlit morning with a dead man huddled in her car.

To hell with her sister.

I smiled and raised my glass. I felt reckless, carefree, happy. I could walk out of here any time. There was a telephone on a small stand in a corner and I could call

Homicide and report a dead man in the rear of a car belonging to Miss Linda Prosper at such and such an address, and walk out of there. That would take care of my obligation to the law.

And Vivian Prosper's request for me to break up the affair between her sister and Arthur Spotwood didn't worry me. I could handle that. Merely a routine matter of checking on Spotwood, finding his weak spot. All men had weak spots, including me. My current weak spot was a blazing red-hot spot for Vivian Prosper. It would be a simple matter to get rid of Spotwood—bribe him, scare him, frame him if I had to. If Vivian Prosper paid me enough I could frame him good. And if he were a cold-blooded fortune hunter, as Vivian Prosper claimed, I would enjoy framing him. But there were other methods, all of them routine for a competent man. And I considered myself a competent man. Fairly competent, anyhow.

But murder was different. Murder is never routine, except in war. I didn't want any part of murder, not even for the promise of paradise. I'm not noble, not me, even if I did belong to the Youth Uplift League when I was in high school, and I wasn't so sexually starved that I could pantingly regard a gorgeous grass widow as a prize to be won no matter what the price. But I was curious to see how far she would go to cover up for her wayward sister.

It was her move, and she made it. I was glad. It brought things out in the open.

"I'm scared," she said softly, and she gazed down at her tightly held glass. "I'm scared for Linda, and for me. And there is no one to help …" She took a slow step toward me.

It was pretty obvious, but I didn't care. For my money she could be as obvious as she wanted. Gently I took her glass from her hand and placed it beside mine on the table. She didn't protest or raise her eyes. I put an arm around her and pulled her to me. She tilted her face upward, her lips half parted, her eyes veiled by silky lashes. I kissed her hard, and her mouth drove against mine. I liked it very much and I didn't want to let her go. Her body stirred contentedly against me.

Presently she pushed her hands against my chest and moved back a trifle. "That—that was rather sudden," she said breathlessly.

"Too sudden?"

She shook her head. Her face held a faint flush, and her eyes were dark and smoky-looking. I reached for her again, but she placed a hand on my arm.

"No—not now."

"When?"

"Later ... maybe."

"No maybe," I said. "When?"

"Will you help me?"

"Help you what? Unload that corpse?"

"Yes."

"No. Not me."

She laughed deep in her throat and stepped into my arms once more. I was willing as long as she was, but no matter how willing she was, I wasn't going to help her bury a dead man, or dump him in the lake for her. But she had different ideas. Just when I was beginning to forget about her problems and to concentrate on her, she pulled her lips away and twisted free of my arms.

"Of course you'll help," she said, "but we must hurry." Her voice was low, urgent, a little thick. "It'll be easy. I know a place along the lake, about five miles from here. There's kind of a cliff there, and the water is deep, and no one lives close. I can do that much for Linda, and after next month, when she's eighteen, she'll be on her own. I promised Mother I'd take care of her until then." She patted my cheek. "In twenty minutes it'll be over. No one will see us, no one will know. But I can't do it alone. I'll pay you—"

"Money can't buy a thing like that," I said.

She said simply, "Did I mention money?"

I began to sweat. I really wanted to help her, but not in the way she wanted to be helped. "You're crazy," I told her. "This is murder. We don't know who he is, where your sister was last night, what happened, how the body got in her car, anything about it. The police may be on their way here now."

She stepped close to me. "Please," she whispered, and her lips moved against my face. "For me. For Linda. It'll be so easy. You'll see. You won't be sorry, I promise. Darling, I promise ..."

The "darling" got me. That did it. It was just the right false note I needed to cool me off fast. I wasn't her darling, and she knew it. I wasn't even a casual cocktail-party acquaintance to whom "darling" would have been an appropriately careless address. I was just a guy she'd met less than an hour before and from whom she wanted a favor. Just a simple little favor like helping her to conceal a corpse. I think she was immediately sorry, and maybe she felt a little like a two-dollar girl on Saturday night. I don't know. But whatever she felt, it must have decided her to regain the lost ground and bring out the heavy artillery. She gave me the works. I let her.

All of her pressed against me, and her fingers dug into my shoulders. "Say you like me," she whispered. "Say it."

"I like you."

"And you'll help me?"

"No."

"Please, please. For me." Her lips moved to a corner of my mouth.

"You can't get away with a thing like that."

"Yes, we can. We can do anything—you and I." Her hands crept upward and pulled my head down and her long body clung and arched inward.

So I kissed her once more. What could I lose? But I shouldn't have pushed my luck so far. Behind us I heard a faint sound and I turned my head.

A man was standing in the doorway. He was smiling.

Chapter Three

Vivian Prosper turned slowly away from me. "We have a doorbell, Arthur," she said in a brittle voice.

The man in the doorway said, "I'm sorry. I saw Linda's car in the drive—and I did knock on the back door. Where's Linda?"

He was about six foot two, husky, blond, with a tanned hard face and clear brown eyes. He was wearing dark blue slacks and a pale blue short-sleeved shirt, open at the neck. There was thick golden hair on his heavy forearms. A cigarette dangled from his lips and there was an amused look in his eyes.

"Linda is sleeping," Vivian Prosper said coldly.

He raised his eyebrows and glanced at a heavy gold wrist watch. "She must have been out late last night." He grinned and added, "Don't look at me that way. She wasn't with me. I came out here to get her car. We've got it scheduled for a grease job and oil change. I figured she'd forgotten and I came to pick it up."

I looked out of the window. A battered jeep was parked in the drive behind Linda Prosper's red convertible. Big white letters on the side of the jeep read: "Spotwood's Super Service." A kid in a white T shirt was behind the wheel.

Vivian Prosper said, "I'll tell Linda you were here. You can get her car later."

"I may as well take it now," he said. "One of the boys will bring it back this afternoon." He turned to go.

"No," Vivian Prosper said sharply.

He turned slowly, a puzzled frown on his tanned face. Looking at him, I could see that he would be attractive to women. Not just to Linda Prosper, but to any woman. Virile was the word for Arthur Spotwood. He had a strong jaw, full mobile mouth with dimples at the corners, and big white teeth. His shoulders were so heavy that they seemed to be bursting from the blue shirt. His thick yellow eyebrows were sun-faded to a pale gold and they stood out sharply against his strong dark face.

"She—she may want to use her car," Vivian Prosper said hurriedly. "She can bring it over later."

"But I can have it back in an hour," he said impatiently. "After all, you said she was sleeping."

"No, no," she said, and she shot me an imploring look. "Don't take it now." There was a faint edge of hysteria in her voice.

"You heard her," I said. "Leave the car here."

He gazed at the two of us, smiling faintly. Then he lifted his wide shoulders and said, "Sure, O.K." He turned abruptly and went out.

Vivian Prosper sighed shakily. "Do you suppose that he …?"

"I don't know," I said, handing her her glass.

She took the drink with a hand that trembled. "Thanks. I need it."

"So that was Arthur Spotwood?"

"Yes."

I moved to the window and gazed down at the drive. Spotwood came out of the house, said something to the kid in the jeep, and moved to the Ford convertible. He walked around it slowly, looking it over.

I said, "Stay here," to Vivian Prosper and I moved quickly out of the room and down the big hall and out to the drive. I put a foot on the brown stain on the

Ford's rear bumper and lit a cigarette. Arthur Spotwood came around from the front of the car and stood looking at it with his hands in his pockets, the cigarette still drooping from his lips.

"Needs a wax job," he said to no one in particular.

"Yeah," I agreed.

"I could take it now, just as well as not," he complained. "It's overdue for service. Linda is pretty careless."

"Big Sister says no," I said.

"Sure," he said bitterly. "What Big Sister says is law."

I glanced around. The only person in sight was the kid in the jeep. He stared at me with a bored expression. I looked up at the library window. Vivian Prosper was standing there watching us. I took a deep drag on my cigarette and said to Spotwood, "Are you sure you weren't with Linda last night?"

"Who the hell are you?" he asked pleasantly.

"A friend of Vivian's."

"So I gathered."

"Stop leering," I told him, "and answer my question. Were you?"

"I don't get it," he said. "About Vivian, I mean. I'm sorry to have busted in on you, but I was pretty surprised. I thought she was a rather cold gal. I mean cold. What did you do to her?" His smile was friendly.

"Nothing," I said modestly. "We're just—friends."

He shook his head. "I still don't get it. Vivian is a man-hater. I thought she hated everything in pants, including me. Most especially me."

"Why?" I asked innocently.

He lifted his heavy shoulders. "How the hell do I know? Maybe it's because of her unhappy marriage, and all that stuff. I'm no psychoanalyst. Maybe she's frustrated or something. But she don't have to take it out on me. Look, you're a friend of hers, aren't you?"

He grinned and added, "Apparently you are, any-how."

"Sure," I said.

"Well, what's she got against me? I mean, other than the fact that I work for a living."

I decided to feel him out a little. "She thinks you were with Linda last night—all night. And Linda came home dead drunk this morning. That's enough to worry any big sister."

It seemed to me that his face took on a gray tinge beneath the tan. He compressed his lips into a straight line. "I don't like that," he said in a tight voice. "I don't like it at all. She's just a kid, and she drinks too much." He kicked at a tire of the convertible and I could see that he was thinking bitter thoughts. Then he jerked his head up. "Who had her out all night? I'll kill the bastard."

"I told you who Vivian *thinks* she was with."

"Vivian is wrong," he snapped. "Sure, I saw Linda last night. I had dinner with her, but I left her right afterward. I had to go back to the station. She said she was going home." He took a deep breath. "She needs somebody to look after her."

"Somebody like you?" I asked.

"You're damn right," he blurted. "If I had my way, we'd get married tomorrow."

I wanted to get his side of the story, and I said, "Why don't you?"

"Hah!" he said bitterly. "Vivian's her legal guardian—until Linda's eighteen—and she won't give her consent. But as soon as Linda is eighteen we can tell Vivian to go to hell and go ahead and get married."

That jibed, approximately, with what Vivian had told me. "Does Linda want to marry you?" I asked him.

For an instant his eyes shifted. "She will," he said firmly. "I—I hope she will. I'm nuts about her."

"It takes two," I said. "Where did you have dinner with her?"

"What is this?" he said. "Is Linda in trouble? What's going on?"

"I told you. Do you have any idea who she might have been with?" I hesitated, and then said, "After she left you, I mean?"

"No," he said evenly. "If I knew, I'd—"

"Yes, yes," I broke in wearily. "You'd kill the bastard. You said that before. Could you make any guesses?"

"Yes, but they would be just guesses."

"Would you care to make some?"

"No. Why did you want to know where we had dinner? And I asked you before—who the hell are you, anyhow?"

"Brice is the name."

Suddenly he smiled and held out his hand. "Call me Art. No need for us to act like a couple of tomcats. It's just that I'm a little touchy about Linda. You asked a reasonable question—we ate at the Village Bar and Grill. It's just a block from my gas station."

We shook hands. Just a couple of pals. "Thanks, Art. Now tell me what Vivian has against you—really."

"She thinks I'm after Linda's money—or rather, the money she'll get."

"Are you?"

We weren't pals anymore. I could see it in his eyes. "I might have known that any friend of Vivian's would be a heel," he said.

"No offense," I said.

He took a quick step toward me, his right fist clenched. I watched him warily, wondering if I'd have to kick him in the stomach. Fists are so futile. A good hefty kick in the right place usually winds things up in a hurry. But I didn't have to kick him.

He stopped and cradled the fist in a palm. "No," he said, as if talking to himself. "Big Sister would just love it if I socked a boy friend of hers. It would make a swell story to tell Linda." He attempted a horrible imitation of a female voice. "That no-good awful roughneck, that grease monkey, that uncouth Art Spotwood, striking my friend Mr. Brice." He turned abruptly away, strode to the jeep, and climbed in beside the kid. The jeep zoomed back down the drive, straightened out, and headed east. I flicked my cigarette across the grass and gazed up at the library window. Vivian Prosper was still standing there. I waggled a couple of fingers at her and walked to the front of the convertible. I took the keys from the ignition switch, locked the trunk compartment, and pocketed the keys. Then I went back into the house, moved down the hall, and entered the library.

Vivian Prosper was standing just inside the door. She was smoking a cigarette and I saw that she had poured herself more Scotch. "What did he say?" she asked quickly.

"He admits that he had dinner with Linda last night, but claims that he left her right afterward and that she said she was going home. He wants to marry her the worst kind of way, and he called me a heel. Why don't you let them get hitched? Let him worry about her. He seems like a sincere, hard-working young man."

"If that's your attitude," she said crisply, "it appears that I'd be wasting my money to hire you to break up the affair."

"My attitude has nothing to do with it. If I take on a job, I do it, regardless of my personal feelings. But it seems to me—"

"I know what's best for my sister," she said sharply.

I shrugged. "O.K. I'll break it up."

Suddenly she smiled. "Do you really mean it?"

"Sure."

She moved close. "Thank you. I—I don't feel so—so alone anymore. Linda has been a terrible worry, a great responsibility. But with you helping me ..." She paused, and then asked quietly, "What do you plan to do?"

I was thinking of a dead man huddled in the rear of a red convertible. That alone should be more than enough to shatter the one-sided romance of Arthur Spotwood with Linda Prosper. "Don't worry about it. There are several methods."

"Maybe it would be best if I didn't know the method?"

"Maybe."

She smiled. "I'll leave it to you. What's your first name?"

"Andy."

She placed her glass on a table and moved past me. At the door she turned and said softly, "Ready, Andy?"

I stood still.

"Please hurry. We can't do anything about Arthur and Linda until we—we take care of this other matter. It won't take long. Then we'll come back here, the two of us, and we'll have a drink and forget about it. You won't be sorry, I promise. If you knew me better, you'd know that I always keep my promises—especially the ones I want to keep."

She was throwing it at me. I was flattered. I couldn't think of anything nicer. I wanted to help her, to do the thing that she wanted me to, but I couldn't and I hated it. I hated it to beat hell. But I hated what she wanted worse. Not that I was afraid, or had any special qualms. In fact, there was a good chance that we could get away with it. It was just that I didn't want to help her dump a corpse in the lake, baby sister or not, luscious promises or not.

I shook my head slowly. "The police have quaint ideas about reporting murders. I've wasted too much time now. But I'll do this much: We'll talk to Linda first. Maybe she can tell us something now." I moved to the door, not looking at her, and entered the hall. Before I reached the stairs she said a word so low that I almost missed it.

"No."

It was the way she said it that made me turn. I don't know where she'd been hiding it, but she held a flat little silver-plated .22 automatic in her hand. It was pointed at a spot just above my belt buckle.

Chapter Four

It was a cute little gun, like a toy, but even a .22 slug could do a lot of damage in the middle of my stomach. I said reproachfully, "You didn't have to do that."

"Linda is my sister," she said in an unsteady voice. "My baby sister. I used to push her around in a carriage, and change her diapers and give her bottles. Mother used to tell me that I was more of a mother to Linda than she was, and I was proud. She was like a doll to me, a live doll, and I promised to take care of her, to keep her from harm. Maybe I haven't done a very good job, but I've tried. I'm still trying. Now she's in trouble—bad trouble—and I've got to help her, somehow. I'm going to get rid of that—that body in her car. I don't know who he is, and I don't want to know. All I know is that I'm going to protect Linda. If I get caught at it—well, things won't be any worse than they are now, and—"

"Like hell they won't," I broke in. I moved toward her.

She backed up, holding the gun steady. I didn't like the tight way her finger was crooked around the trigger, or the determined look in her eyes. A woman, any woman, with a gun in her hand is dangerous. I gave her what I hoped was a friendly disarming smile. "You really think that getting rid of that body will help your sister, don't you?"

"Of course."

"No other reason?"

"I'm thinking of Linda—just Linda."

I lifted my arms in a resigned manner. "I think you're asking for trouble, but if it's what you want ..."

A gleam of hope flared in her eyes. "You'll help me?"

I smiled at her. "It'll cost you plenty."

She uttered a small sigh of relief and the muzzle of the gun dropped a little. That was what I was waiting for. I jumped for her and my fingers closed over her wrist. She didn't struggle or cry out, but let me take the gun from her limp fingers. I stepped away from her. I felt a little silly. It had been too easy.

She gazed at me with tears in her eyes. "I—I believed you."

"I'm sorry," I said, and I clicked open the breech of the gun and removed the small cartridge clip. Both breech and clip were empty. I held the empty clip in my hand and looked at her.

"Of course," she said. "I knew it was empty. I hate guns." She turned away and began to sob quietly.

I stared at her helplessly. First kisses and promises of more than kisses, then a gun pointed at me, now tears. Women. I dropped the little gun into my coat pocket, stepped up behind her, and placed my hands on her shoulders. Beneath the thin sweater her skin felt soft and warm. "Take it easy," I said. "Maybe it'll work out. I'll do all I can to help."

She turned slowly within the circle of my arms. "Hold me," she whispered. "Just hold me for a minute. I—I'll be all right."

I held her, hoping that nobody would walk in on us. Nobody did, and presently she stirred and lifted her head. Her eyes were wet. "Thanks," she said. "I'm fine now. Do you forgive me—about the gun?"

"Sure—as long as it wasn't loaded."

She sighed, took a handkerchief from a pocket of the slacks, and dabbed at her eyes. "I'm just jittery, I guess." She moved away from me to the stairs. "You were right. Let's talk to Linda."

I followed her up the stairs.

Linda Prosper looked very small and dark against the white sheets on the big bed. They had put blue silk pajamas on her. She lay quietly on her side, breathing heavily. Her dark brown hair clung damply to her forehead and there was sweat on her face. The fat little maid stood at one end of the room twisting her hands together.

Vivian Prosper leaned over the bed. "Linda, honey, can you hear me? Feeling better?"

She didn't move. Her labored breathing filled the room. I glanced at Vivian Prosper and I saw the worry and the fear in her eyes. I looked once more at the girl on the bed. I didn't like what I saw.

"Linda," Vivian said in a sharp whisper.

The maid made a small whimpering sound.

I leaned down and with a thumb and forefinger. I lifted one of the girl's eyelids. The eye stared at me blankly, like a glass eye, unseeing. The pupil was contracted to a tiny pin point. I placed a finger on her throat. The blood was moving very feebly through her veins. I looked up at Vivian Prosper. She was watching me silently, her eyes wide, her lips parted.

"Call a doctor—now," I snapped. "She's been doped."

Things moved fast around the Prosper household. A tall, bald-headed doctor arrived ten minutes after Vivian's call and shooed me out of the bedroom. I went down to the library and called Detective Sergeant Dave Navarre. I didn't tell him any more than I had to, and I hung up before he could ask too many questions. I wanted a little time to think things over before the serious questioning began. The bar in the library didn't tempt me while I waited. I was no longer in the mood for a drink. I stood by the window and smoked and gazed down at the innocent-looking red Ford convertible in the drive.

It took sixteen minutes for Navarre to get there. That was good time across town in the traffic. The black and white police car slid softly to a stop in the drive behind the convertible. Navarre and a couple of plain-clothes men got out. I went down to meet them. Navarre was a tall, thin, dark man with hollow cheeks, a thin blade of a nose, large liquid brown eyes, and a wide friendly mouth. I had never seen him wear anything but a well-tailored gray flannel suit, a soft white shirt with a button-down collar, and a maroon knit tie. It was like a uniform, winter and summer. His only concession to the seasons, as far as I knew, was that in the summer he switched from a brown, snap-brim hat to a Panama. He was wearing the Panama now, with a dark blue band. He said, "Hello, Andy. Bit off a big chunk this time, huh?" He had a deep pleasant voice.

"You said it." I handed him the keys to the Ford and nodded at the trunk. "In there."

He opened the compartment, looked long and intently. The two plain-clothes men peeked around him. Presently Navarre said, "All right, boys, watch it." He turned to me, jerked a thumb toward the swimming pool, and moved away. I followed him. We sat on an iron bench near the edge of the pool. A rubber raft floated about five feet from the end of the diving board.

"All right, Andy," he said. "Start from the beginning." I told him all of it—or almost all of it. I didn't tell him about the lapse of time between the moment I found the body and the moment I phoned him, or Vivian Prosper's wild idea about dumping the body. I felt a little uneasy about it because I knew from bitter and embarrassing experience that it never pays to hold back information from the law. A homicide cop is a pretty smart boy, and I have nothing but respect for cops in general, Dave Navarre in particular. But I had a client to protect, at least until such time as I decided that she didn't deserve protection, if that time came, and I figured that my little omissions wouldn't affect Navarre's immediate course of action. Anyhow, I hoped they wouldn't.

When I had finished, he said, "Very good, Andy. That's a complete picture. Will you take me to the older sister now?"

He used the radio phone in the police car before we went inside. I introduced him to Vivian and he removed his Panama and was very polite and soft-spoken. Then he and Vivian went upstairs. I heard Navarre speaking to the doctor, and a door closed quietly. I wandered into the library, decided that I still didn't want another drink, and moved to the window. The two plain-clothes men were sitting on the rear bumper of the convertible. The door of the trunk compartment was closed. One of them got up and began to walk slowly up and down the drive. The other lit a cigarette and stared off into space. If I didn't know Navarre, I would have thought it looked more like a wake than a murder investigation.

I had almost made up my mind to have another drink of Vivian Prosper's Scotch when I heard voices on the stairs. I went out into the hall. Navarre and the doctor, talking earnestly, were coming down the steps.

They reached the hall and the doctor said something emphatically, waving his hands, and Navarre nodded gravely. Then the doctor picked up his hat from a hall table and went out the front door. He didn't look at me as he passed.

Navarre came toward me. He didn't look like a detective of police. He looked like a college professor, or an artist, or maybe an actor. He gave me his friendly smile. "The doctor says she'll pull out of it. When she can talk maybe we'll know a few answers."

I held up my glass. "Drink, Dave? It belongs to the Prosper family, but I'm sure you're welcome."

He shook his head. "I'm a sundown drinker. Are you still working for the older sister?"

"I don't know. This may change the picture."

He gave me his grave smile. "If you should snoop around for her—on either the romance breakup or the killing—I assume that I can count on your usual cooperation and tact?"

"Sure. Can I count on yours?"

"Within limits, Andy. You know that. Right now the main thing is to keep it quiet. I don't want any newspaper publicity—not until that body is identified."

"Right, Sergeant." I moved to the window. Two more police cars and a black ambulance were now in the drive and a number of men were moving about in a businesslike manner—the medical examiner, the flash-bulb boys, the little efficient men with the fingerprint equipment. I peered out toward the street. Three uniformed cops were keeping a gathering crowd at bay. I said to Navarre, "You already have publicity."

He moved across the room and stood beside me. "Vultures," he said in a surprisingly harsh voice. "They probably smelled the blood." He sighed. "Well, we can't help that. It still won't be in the papers." He turned and moved to the door. "See you later, Andy."

In a minute I saw him emerge on the drive. Two of the technicians came up and began talking to him.

I heard a small sound behind me and I turned. Vivian Prosper came in and sat down in a lemon-yellow chair. She was pale and her lips needed repainting, but she still looked marvelous.

"How's Linda?" I asked her.

"Didn't Sergeant Navarre tell you?"

"He said she'd pull out of it, but he didn't give me any details, and I didn't ask."

"She's much better, but she might have died—if it hadn't been for you." She shivered slightly and hugged her knees. "Morphine poisoning. An overdose, with a hypo. She had been drinking a lot, too, and there's a nasty bruise on the back of her head." She stood up and moved to the telephone. "I suppose I'd better try to locate Jerome," she said wearily.

She called six numbers, but she didn't locate him. I finished the Scotch and placed my glass carefully on a table. She cradled the phone abruptly and said under her breath, "To hell with it." She swung toward me. "Well, you working for me or not?"

"It's your money," I said. "If you still want me, I'll do what I can."

"Very well," she said briskly, like a vice-president's secretary. "The important thing now is to get Linda out of this mess. It's very obvious that Sergeant Navarre is linking her with that man's death."

"Naturally," I said. "After all—"

"I know, I know," she broke in impatiently. "I want to find proof that will clear her."

"What if I find proof that she's in it up to her neck?"

"I've thought of that," she snapped. "But it might help if I know it before the police do."

"We might try talking to Linda before Navarre does."

She laughed shortly. "You don't know Linda. She'll never tell us anything she doesn't want us to know."

"She'll have to give some kind of story sooner or later."

She began to pace around the room. I watched her. She was a girl who knew her attractions, and she knew that I was aware of them. She stopped before the big window where the early-afternoon sunlight fell on her to the best advantage. It glinted on her pale yellow hair and cast pleasing shadows over her long-legged figure in the white sweater and the smooth-fitting slacks. When she turned to face me the reflected sun made a soft glow on her face and changed her eyes into a blue deeper than the sky behind her. "A while ago you kissed me," she said quietly. "You made love to me. I encouraged you brazenly, because I wanted you to like me enough to do something for me. It was—was cheap of me, but I was thinking of my sister. You wouldn't do what I wanted, and I see now that you were right. I think I admire you, and I feel now that I can trust you. I want you to forget what has happened—I mean, between us. From now it's to be a strictly business arrangement. Is that clear?"

"Yes," I said, "but I liked it better the way it was."

"Oh, stop it," she said sharply. "Stop trying to revive the illusion of love. You're a grown man, and you surely know better."

"Yes, ma'am," I said. "I am to try to learn what happened last night, how that corpse got in your sister's car. A strictly business deal. I do a job for you and you pay me—in money. O.K. Now, what about Arthur Spotwood? Do I understand that you want me to work on him, too?"

"Yes. I strongly suspect that he's mixed up in Linda's trouble. The important thing is to get Linda cleared of any implication of murder, and the second most important thing is to see that Arthur Spotwood stops hanging around her. I don't care how much it costs or how long it takes. My duty is to Linda. She comes before everything else. Do you understand, Mr. Brice?"

"Yes, ma'am, I understand perfectly." If she wanted to be formal, I could be formal as hell too.

A door slammed at the front end of the hall.

Vivian Prosper said, "That's Jerome. He always slams the door."

A big heavy man walked into the room. He had a fleshy sunburned face, a short thick nose, three sagging chins, and black eyes magnified to the size of ping-pong balls behind thick lenses in wide brown-mottled frames. He was wearing a pearl-gray summer suit, a dazzling orange silk tie, no hat.

He had hair, but it was all around his ears. The top of his bald head was sunburned. He glanced briefly at me, dismissed me, and said to Vivian in a rich baritone, "What in hell is going on out there? Cars in the drive, cops, people. I had to tell a guy who I was before I could come into my own house."

"Jerome," she said, "Linda is in trouble. Bad trouble. I tried to call you, but—"

"Trouble?" he barked. "Linda is always in trouble. A high-spirited girl. Got to expect that. She'll settle down. What's that got to do with that damned crowd in my driveway?" Before she could answer, he looked at me and said, "I don't seem to recall meeting you, sir."

Vivian said, "This is Mr. Brice. He's a private detective, working for me. Linda was gone all night, and she came home this morning with a dead man in her car. The police are investigating it."

He had poured himself a stiff drink of bourbon and was in the act of drinking it, straight. "What?" he sputtered, lowering his glass.

She told him quickly in an ice-cold voice what had happened, all of it, including the reason she had called me in the first place. When she had finished, Jerome

Pitt finished his drink and poured another, the neck of
the bourbon bottle rattling nervously against the glass.
He took a long swallow, no chaser, before he spoke.
Then he said in a pompous voice, "Preposterous, ridic-
ulous," and he pointed a wavering finger at me. "Get
rid of this—this person immediately. He can serve no
good purpose, and you had no right to proceed in the
highhanded manner you have. I trusted you to keep
Linda out of trouble, and you have failed me. And as
for Arthur Spotwood, I think that Linda is old enough
to pick her friends without interference from you. After all, your marriage was a failure, and you have no
right to meddle in Linda's private affairs."

"Thank you, Jerome," she said. "Thank you very
much."

"Damn it," he shouted, "it's the truth. You're jealous of Linda—always have been. You don't want her
to have any happiness." He paused, glaring, and then
added in a milder tone, "I'll admit that she's too wild
for a girl her age. But she'll get over it. She's more like
your mother than you ever were. She'll come out all
right—if you just let her alone. And as for this—this
fantastic occurrence, I am sure there is a logical explanation. Perhaps Linda's car was used as a hiding place
for a gang killing, something like that. It has nothing
to do with her, or with us. Let the police handle the
silly business. As a matter of fact, I'll speak to the
Commissioner about it. Good friend of mine." He
fixed me with a beady eye. "And as for this so-called
detective, I demand that you discharge him immediately." He finished his whisky in one long swallow and
poured more into his glass.

"I am paying for Mr. Brice's services with my own
money," Vivian Prosper said in a hard, cold voice. "He
stays."

Jerome Pitt swung toward her. His heavy face was
congested and blotched-looking. "Then you can damn
well get out of my house," he shouted. "I won't stand

for this sort of cops-and-robbers nonsense. If you are foolish enough to squander your mother's legacy on a cheap keyhole peeper, I can't stop you. But by God, I don't have to stand around and watch you do it."

I winked at Vivian Prosper, but she didn't see me, and I guessed that she wasn't in a winking mood. Her face was gray beneath the tan.

"*Your* house?" she said in a low, intense voice. "It's your house only because Mother left it to you—it and the money for your hunting and fishing and your clubs and your gambling and your liquor and your women. Linda's my sister, and I'm trying to help her. If I leave this house, Linda goes with me."

He roared like a lion goaded with a pitchfork. "Goddamn it, you can't do that! She's my legal step-daughter. I'll fight you to the last ditch, Vivian, I'm warning you." He took another gulp of whisky and immediately began to choke on it.

Vivian Prosper stared at him contemptuously.

I caught her eye then and jerked my head at the door. She followed me out to the hall, her face still pale with anger. From the library we could hear Jerome Pitt's spasmodic coughing.

"I hope he strangles," she said.

"Forget him," I told her. "Let's see if we can talk to Linda."

She nodded and followed me up the stairs.

Chapter Five

The fat little maid came out of Linda Prosper's room. "She's awake now," she said to Vivian in a hushed voice. "She seems much better. I gave her the medicine the doctor left."

We entered the bedroom. Linda's small face looked very pale against her dark hair spread out on the pillow. "Hi," she said weakly to her sister, and her gaze strayed to me. "Who's the boy friend?"

"This is Mr. Brice. He wants to ask you a few questions—about last night."

The girl on the bed smiled faintly. "Shoot," she said.

I said, "Tell us what you remember about last night and this morning. All of it."

"Why, sure." She gazed up at the ceiling and put a small forefinger to her plump lower lip. "Well, now, let's see. First I had dinner with Arthur. He had to get back to his old gas station, and so I chaperoned a kiddy party at the Ebenezer Welfare Association. Then I had a pineapple soda with two lovely ladies from the Anti-Saloon Crusaders, and after that I attended an extremely stimulating lecture on juvenile delinquency at the Hearts and Flowers Bachelor Girls Club. Oh, I had a very busy evening. When I left the bachelor girls it was way past nine o'clock and I came straight home to my beddy-bye." She looked up at me with wide, innocent eyes.

Vivian said harshly, "Listen, you little fool. You came home at ten o'clock this morning dead drunk and shot full of morphine, and you damn near died. And there was a dead man in the trunk of your car. Now try to give us a silly story about *that.*"

Linda said to me, "Isn't she beautiful when she's mad?"

I said, "Look, miss. This is really serious. Your sister has told you just the way it is. The police are here, and you will probably be under arrest before tonight. You tell us the truth and we'll do all we can to help you."

She gazed at me coolly, looking me over, and her eyes held a look that no seventeen-year-old eyes should ever have. "You mean I'll be arrested for *murder?* Oh,

what fun! That will really be something new." She
turned her face away. "Go away, quickly, both of you.
You bore me."

Vivian Prosper gave me a helpless look.

I said to Linda, "If you won't talk to us, you'll have
to talk to the police. Make up your mind and take your
choice."

She turned her head and gazed at me thoughtfully.
Then she put a finger to her mouth like a six-year-old
caught with her hand in the cookie jar. "I'll talk to
you," she said wistfully. "Alone."

I glanced at Vivian Prosper. She hesitated a second.
Then she turned abruptly and went out, leaving the
door open. I heard her steps on the stairs.

Linda said, "Hell with her. She's just jealous. She
thinks I try to take her boy friends away from her."

"Do you?"

"Of course. It's fun." Her fingers plucked at the
silken cover. "You're cute. Are you new?"

"Pretty new. Only slightly tarnished."

She giggled. "You're new to me. I think I like you
better than her last boy friend. You have more hair.
Are you in love with her? I mean really? Passionately?"

"Not yet."

"Don't waste your time. She's cold. I'm much nicer,
and I'm not cold. Would you like me to show you?"

"Not now," I said. "Just tell me what happened last
night."

She wiggled on the bed and pushed herself to a sitting position. The silken cover slid down and I saw that
the front of her pajamas was unbuttoned. She didn't
seem to notice, but maybe she did, and I most certainly
did, and I lit a cigarette to cover the fact that I was
trying not to notice. Both of the Prosper sisters, I
thought, were decidedly gifted.

She said, "There's an ash tray on the table behind
you."

"Thanks." I reached around and placed the ash tray on my knee. She plucked at her pajama top modestly, pulling it together. Then she held out a hand and the jacket fell open again.

"May I please have a cigarette?" she asked.

"No, you may not. You aren't old enough to smoke."

"I am too old enough." She pouted. "I'm old enough for a lot of things."

"Like what?"

"Oh, like having a drink, and going with boys, and staying out late, and driving a car, and—"

"And murder?" I broke in.

Her big brown eyes got bigger. The dark pupils were still tiny dots from the morphine. "That's a funny thing to say."

"Murder is always funny. Who is he?"

"Who?"

"The dead man in the back of your car."

For an instant I thought her eyes wavered, but I could have been wrong. "Is he handsome?" she asked.

"He was, before he got dead. About twenty-three, black hair cut short, blue eyes, scar on his nose. Know him?"

She avoided my gaze and plucked at the cover. "He—he sounds very attractive, but must we talk about dead people?"

"We must."

She sighed and closed her eyes. The pajama jacket was still hanging open. "Close the door," she said.

"Your sister can't hear us. She went downstairs."

"You don't know her. She probably sneaked back up and is listening outside. She's jealous of me. She hates me. She's always hated me. I'm cuter than she is, and she doesn't like it. She was Mother's favorite and she can't get over it. So I take her boy friends away from her and I laugh." She opened her eyes and there was a hot glint in them. "I'll show her."

I wasn't interested in a clinical history of the Prosper family, or in the psychological damage resulting from the concentration of maternal love. I said, "If I close the door, will you tell me everything that happened last night?"

"Yes."

I got up, moved to the door, and peeked up and down the hall. If Vivian Prosper was lurking about, she was under the rug or behind one of the closed doors. I shut the door to Linda's room and returned to the chair by the bed. I wished I had a drink. I wished I was the hell out of there, even downstairs with Vivian discussing things on a strictly business basis. I knew I wasn't going to do any good here with little Linda. I knew it before she squirmed eagerly out of bed and flung herself into my lap.

Her arms curled around me and she buried her face against my neck. I smelled a faint perfume, the bitter smell of medicine, and the dying reek of whisky. Her small body trembled a little. "Hold me," she whispered. "I'm scared."

I was scared too, scared that Vivian would walk in on us. "All right," I said. "I'm holding you. Now tell me about it."

She stopped trembling and her body was suddenly soft and clinging. "Don't you like me better than Vivian?" she murmured.

"Sure. I'm crazy about you. Now talk. Talk about last night."

Her arms tightened around me. "Must we?" she asked in a muffled voice. "Can't it wait—just a little?"

"No. You promised me if I closed the door—"

"Isn't it cozy in here with the door closed?"

"Just a couple of bugs in a rug," I said. "But Vivian—"

"Stop," she cut in. "Stop talking about Vivian. She was Mother's pet, and I was just a tag-along. She had the prettiest clothes, the fanciest birthday parties, the cutest boys. I wore her worn-out hand-me-down dresses, and played with her castoff toys. She used to take me to the park in a pushcart and leave me bawling while she played with other kids on the slides and the teeter-totters. And when she was sixteen and I was nine, and boys came to the house, she would make fun of me and tell the boys that I was her baby sister. I'd run away crying and she'd laugh and the boys thought she was wonderful. Don't talk to me about my darling sister."

She sat up straight and there were tears in her eyes. "Talk about me," she pleaded. "I'm nice, too. Nicer than Vivian. See?" She placed her hands on my face and kissed me. Her small mouth was soft and cool.

I pushed her away from me. I wasn't rough, but I was firm. The Prosper sisters' brand of teasing come-on was beginning to bore me a little. I liked the women, sure, but Vivian's hot-and-cold act had left me a little frustrated, and I wasn't in the mood to play games with Linda. I grabbed her shoulders and held her out where I could look at her. The pajama jacket had slipped half off of her, but I didn't pay any attention. "Goddamn it, what did you do last night?" I almost shouted at her.

"You don't have to swear," she said demurely, her eyes downcast. She made no move to pull up the pajama jacket.

I shook her and I wasn't gentle. "Tell me."

She gazed at the ceiling and said dreamily, "Well, let's see. I chaperoned a kiddy party, and then I had a pineapple soda with—"

I stood up and dumped her on the bed. "Button your pajamas," I snarled, and strode to the door and jerked it open. Her low mocking laughter followed me into the hall.

I didn't slam the door. I remembered in time that Vivian was probably listening below, and I closed it in a dignified manner.

She wasn't listening. She was sitting alone in the library with a drink in her hand. "Any luck?" she asked.

I shook my head. "She needs a good paddling."

She sighed. "I know. What now?"

I shrugged.

"Would you like a drink?"

"No, thanks."

"And you're working for me?"

"Yes, if that's what you want."

"I do. I told you that."

I moved to the door.

"Will I see you soon?" she asked.

"I'll call you."

"All right."

I went out. It was a hell of a conversation, but I guess that was the way we both felt. I moved down the hall.

Jerome K. Pitt ambushed me beneath the stairs. He stepped out from the semidarkness, placed a finger to his lips, and motioned to me silently. I followed him to the door at the end of the hall. He looked up and down and over each shoulder. Then he pressed something into my hand. It felt like money. I looked at it in the dim light. It was money. Four fifties.

He looked again over his shoulder, like a man about to tell a story he didn't want the ladies to hear. Then he leaned close and said in a hoarse whisper, "Keep it, Brice. It's yours. Arthur Spotwood is a fine young man. Be a good thing if Linda married him. Just forget about that deal with Vivian, and let the police handle this silly business of that—that body in her car. Do you understand?" It seemed to me that he was trembling a little.

I looked down at the money in my hand. "I'm just a cheap keyhole peeper," I murmured. "I'm afraid—"

He waved a hand impatiently. "Forget what I said. I apologize. I was wrought up. Is it a deal?"

"Well …" I said, with what I was certain was a fake show of reluctance.

He put a heavy hand on my arm. "Good, good," he whispered. "Fine. But no tricks, now."

I winked at him, put the money in my pocket, and went out.

The Venice Café was just a so-so place about two miles beyond the city limits. There was a big cinder parking area, the usual neon sign, and the usual glass block wall on one side. I parked in the rear, walked around to the front, and went in. The place was dusky and cool, and the smell of beer, lemons, and frying fish mixed with the air-conditioning. A juke box twanged away at the far end and eight or ten couples jiggled around on the tiny dance floor. A big lighted clock on the wall back of the bar told me that it was one-thirty in the afternoon, and I realized that I was hungry.

I sat down in one of the booths along the wall. A chunky brunette in a white uniform came over and tossed a menu on the table. She wore too much lipstick and the red lacquer on her fingernails was chipped.

I said, "Double Manhattan, and skip the cherries."

"Do you wish to order lunch, sir?"

"Bring me the drink and I'll decide."

She moved away, swinging her hips slightly more than was necessary. The uniform was too tight for her and she wasn't wearing a girdle. I looked over the menu, decided on the perch and French-fried potatoes, lit a cigarette, and leaned back in the booth. The place was full of people, just people, all shapes and sizes, with mostly men at the long bar.

The brunette brought my drink. "There you are, sir."

"I'll have the perch," I said.

"Yes, sir." She scribbled on a pad and moved away.

I fished a five-dollar bill from my pocket and waited for her to come back with my lunch. She returned in a couple of minutes, but without my lunch. "Are you Mr. Brice?" she asked.

I was startled. "Yeah. Why?"

"You're wanted on the phone. Middle booth, in the rear."

"Me?"

"Yes, sir, Mr. Brice, they said. Black hair, blue suit, blue eyes. That's you."

I didn't understand it, but I said, "Thanks," put the five-dollar bill back in my pocket, and walked back to the middle phone booth. Numbers one and three were occupied, a man in one, a woman in the other, their backs toward me. I picked up the receiver. "Yes?"

A strange shrill voice said, "Mr. Brice?" I couldn't tell if it was a man or a woman.

"Yes."

"Just a moment. Miss Vivian Prosper wishes to speak to you."

I waited for maybe three minutes, wishing that I'd brought my drink with me. Then I jiggled the receiver cradle impatiently. A crisp female voice said, "Your party has left the line, sir."

I cursed softly under my breath, hung up, and went back to my booth. What did Vivian Prosper want, and how did she know that I was at the Venice Café? And who belonged to the odd shrill voice? The fat little maid? I thought, a little dubiously, that maybe Linda had talked to Vivian after I'd left and told her that she'd been at the Venice Café. Or maybe Navarre, after his men found the match folder, had put the pressure on Linda and had got her to talk to him. But who had called me, and why had he, or she, hung up? I lifted my glass and moodily downed the double Manhattan in three slow swallows. It had a queer bitter taste, and I guessed that the Venice Café bartender had used too much Angostura.

The brunette came over and placed plates in front of me. Perch, French fries, tartar sauce in a little paper cup, soft Italian bread, a steaming cup of thick black coffee. "Cream? Sugar?" she asked.

I shook my head, got out the five-dollar bill again, folded it lengthwise. She watched me with an interested expression.

I said, "Does a little dark girl who drives a red Ford convertible come in here often?"

Her gaze was glued to the money in my hand. "Would her name be Linda?" she asked.

I had hit the jackpot. "It would." I handed her the bill. "Was she in here last night?"

She tucked the money into a pocket of her uniform. "Yes," she said.

I gazed at her admiringly. "You're a fine girl, honey. You know that?"

"Aw, go on," she said. She almost wiggled, like a collie when you pat its head and say, "Good dog."

"Who was with her?" I asked.

"Just a couple of guys."

"Know their names?" I was beginning to get excited.

"One of them, the young one, she called him Honey. The other one—he was sort of older—she called him Darling."

"Thanks," I said. "Now tell me what they looked like." She smiled at me and said pleasantly, "I'm supposed to be taking care of the other customers."

I laid two half dollars on the table. I didn't feel so good. The place seemed to be getting darker, and my head ached suddenly. And I was having a little trouble getting breath into my lungs. I saw the brunette's hand, with the chipped nail polish, pick up the half dollars, and she began to talk. But it seemed to me that her voice was booming at me from down a long dark tunnel.

"The young one," she was saying, "the one she called Honey, he was kinda cute. Dark, good-looking, short haircut … blue eyes … scar across his nose …"

Scar across his nose, scar across his nose, scar … The words seemed to ring in my ears like hammer strokes, and the Venice Café swayed up and down in great looping rolls. My head felt as heavy as a bowling ball and abruptly my nose was in my plate. I smelled the hot fried perch, the tartar sauce, and the oil on the potatoes, and there was a fierce hot stabbing pain in my throat.

I tried to speak, but my tongue felt as thick as the thumb of a first baseman's mitt, and I struggled to lift my face from the fish, but I couldn't make it. I heard my glass tinkle to the floor and the alarmed squeal of the waitress was a faraway sound. Then I didn't hear anything or know anything and I didn't care.

Chapter Six

From somewhere in the darkness an anxious voice said, "Feel better now, maybe?"

A second voice said, "You'd better clean up your place, Guido. I'd hate to tip off the Health Department. It looks like ptomaine."

The first voice said excitedly, "But, Doctor! Guido's place is spotless. You eat here yourself. Guido is proud of its spotlessness. He did not get it here, the ptomaine. I know what that is, and I shudder. Never, never in Guido's place. He did not get it here, I swear by the Virgin. He got it down the road, at O'Brian's—O'Brian is very careless about his pots and pans and his garbage—or in the city. He had only one drink here. I check with Pablo and with Blanche. He did not touch the perch or anything. He just passed out—whoom!"

I felt a cool dry hand on my forehead, and the second voice said, "Shush. He's coming around."

I opened my eyes. I saw a low ceiling of cracked rose-tinted plaster, and I moved my head. I was lying on a sagging leather couch in a small room with Venetian blinds at the windows. Cases of beer were stacked along one wall. There were a small cluttered desk, an ancient typewriter, and three green metal files. A wine bottle stood on top of one of the files. The label was pale green and I made out the words "Dry Vermouth." Behind the bottle, on the wall, was tacked a huge calendar with a lush color painting of a naked blonde reclining on a white bearskin rug. The blonde held the inevitable telephone to her red lips and there was a teasing faraway expression in her eyes. Her legs were impossibly long and her breasts were impossibly large and firm. I had a bitter taste in my mouth and my head pounded wickedly. My throat felt as though a ball bat had been rammed down it. I felt dizzy and sick, but everything in the room seemed to be in extraordinarily sharp focus.

A man was standing at the foot of the couch. He was big and brown-skinned with bright black eyes and a Zulu mop of kinky black hair, gray over his ears. Another man stood gazing down at me. He was tall and thin and old, with a narrow pale face and thin hair the color of shaved ice.

This man, the thin one, smiled down at me. It was a nice smile, friendly and compassionate, and it was a real smile, because it showed in his eyes. He wore a wrinkled seersucker suit and an old-fashioned black string tie. The suit was spotted and his soft white shirt was overdue at the laundry. "Welcome back," he said, smiling.

"To where?" I asked. My voice was hoarse and it hurt me to speak. I felt my throat with cautious fingers.

"To the world," he said gently. "To the land of the living. I hope you want to be here." He had a soft

pleasing voice, with only the faintest of whisky rasp.
"You almost left it."

"Thanks," I croaked. "I want to be here."

"Why?" he asked sadly.

I was bewildered, lost in a dark forest. "I don't
know," I said vaguely. "I just had a drink...."

The Zulu man at the foot of the couch waved his
arms wildly. "A Manhattan cocktail," he said excitedly. "What is that? Just a cocktail, a standard cocktail; we serve hundreds every day. The Martini is first
choice of my patrons, the Manhattan is second. Pablo,
my bartender on duty now, he prides himself on his
cocktails, especially the Manhattan. He stirs them ever
so gently, never shakes them, so as not to bruise the
ingredients—you see? Just two parts bonded Bourbon
whisky, one part Italian vermouth, just a leetle dash of
bitters, stir gently in the ice, and then pour in a chilled
glass over a cherry. That is Pablo's Manhattan. Nothing more, I swear it."

The thin man with the shaved-ice hair said gently,
"Stop, Guido, please. You're making me thirsty, and I
have patients to see this afternoon." He touched my
shoulder lightly with a bony finger. "Eat lightly for a
few days, sir."

"Don't worry about it, Doctor," I said. "I always
pass out after a double Manhattan."

He gave me a sad smile. "As good an explanation
as any. That will be five dollars, please."

I pushed myself to a sitting position. My head
pounded and my throat ached, and I felt like hell. But
I managed to get a five-dollar bill from my pocket and
hand it to him. His thin fingers twitched it deftly away,
and he nodded gravely. "Thank you, sir." There was a
short pause, and he cleared his throat. "Uh—there is a
slight additional charge of two dollars and a half for
the use of the stomach pump. Guido, with extraordi-
nary foresight, instructed me to bring it when he called
me."

"A stomach pump?" I asked, feeling my throat.

He inclined his head. "It was disagreeable, but necessary."

I handed him another five. "Keep it, Doctor. And thanks."

He gave me a little courteous bow. "Thank *you*, sir. If you should require my services further, I am Dr. Otten, and my phone number is Lakeside two-o-nine-eight."

"Thanks."

He hesitated. "Don't you wish to note the number?"

"I'll remember."

He gave me a grave sad smile, picked up a battered and ancient black leather bag from the floor, and moved carefully to the door. As he passed the desk he removed a sun-yellowed stiff straw hat from its cluttered surface and placed it on his head at a forward-tilted angle. At the door he turned slowly and with his gentle gaze on the Venetian blinds he said quietly, "Good day, gentlemen." He went out, closing the door softly.

I said to the man with the Zulu cut, "Is he drunk?"

He flashed a mouthful of white teeth at me. "Dr. Otten? He is always drunk. Does it matter?"

"Hell, no. He's a fine gentleman." Tenderly I probed my neck with a thumb and forefinger. "Even with a stomach pump."

He leaned toward me and said anxiously, "Perhaps you had something to eat or drink at O'Brian's before you came to Guido's?"

"No," I said. "Forget it." I placed my feet carefully on the floor and stood up. I swayed a little, but I managed to stay upright. I felt in my pockets for some money and my fingers closed over the two hundred dollars Jerome K. Pitt had given me. I peeled off one of the fifties and handed it to Guido. "Give me another one of Pablo's Manhattans," I told him, "and forty

dollars change. Thanks for thinking of the stomach
pump."

He gave me a puzzled, incredulous look. Then he
threw back his big head and laughed. "I like that,
meester—a gracious gesture. You shall have it, a Manhattan supreme, the flower of Pablo's art." He looked
down at the bill in his hand and added, "And forty
dollars change."

I should have snooped around a little and ques-
tioned the brunette waitress. But I didn't see her
around, and I didn't feel up to it anyhow. It worried
me a little, because a detective is supposed to do things
like that. I sat a little shakily on a bar stool and Pablo,
a swarthy little man with gold teeth, made me a Manhattan supreme with much flourish and delicate stirring. It tasted just like any other mass-production
Manhattan, but after I drank it I sailed out of the Venice Café like a rowboat under forty feet of canvas.

It was three o'clock in the afternoon. I sat in my car
with my hands on the wheel and waited for the Manhattan in my empty stomach to stop working on me.
The cars belonging to the Venice Café customers had
thinned out and the parking area was almost deserted,
waiting for the pre-dinner drinking crowd to fill it up.
The hot sun bounced off the paint of my car hood and
I squinted my eyes against the glare. There wasn't any
breeze and I heard the buzz of crickets from a nearby
thicket. I began to sweat. I got out, took off my coat,
laid it on the rear seat. Then I loosened my tie, lit a
cigarette, and got once more behind the wheel. Cars
on the highway beyond sped past with a sticky
whooshing sound.

After a while a faint breeze came up and I stopped
sweating. At last there were only two cars left in the
parking area and the Venice Café seemed to drowse in
the hot afternoon sun. I lit another cigarette. It tasted
terrible, but it didn't make me sick, and I smoked it,
fighting the taste, as people do, until it was finished.

Then I took a deep breath, pushed the starter button, and circled slowly until I hit the highway. I drove slowly and carefully at a sedate thirty-five miles an hour. It took me an hour and a half to make it to my apartment on the east side of town.

I took a tepid shower, put on a pair of pajama pants, ate two slices of dry toast, and drank a glass of milk. The milk and the toast stayed down and almost immediately I felt better, but it seemed that my arms and legs weighed a hundred pounds each. I stretched out on my bed and the whole damned day faded into nothingness ...

A faraway ringing sound penetrated the thick blanket of sleep. I fought it for a while, but at last I got up and groped for the phone.

"Yeah?" I said stupidly.

A soft female voice said, "I was just about to hang up."

"Why didn't you?" I said nastily with the bed beckoning alluringly behind me.

"All right," the voice said sharply. "I will."

I knew it was Vivian Prosper then, and I said hastily, "No, wait. I guess I'm still asleep."

"At eight o'clock in the evening?" she said mockingly. "I thought that three in the morning was the accepted bedtime for private detectives."

I winced. I wished people wouldn't call me that, and for the umpteenth time I wished that I'd picked some standard, everyday occupation, like a bank clerk, or a vice-president of something, or an insurance salesman, or maybe a drill-press operator. But I didn't know anything else, I wasn't trained for anything else. It was a living, and I didn't have a boss to give me a dirty look when I punched in two minutes late in the morning. Every once in a while I thought of changing the title of my occupation to something like Personal Consultant, or Director of Human Relations, or maybe to the A. J. Brice Personal Problem Bureau. Any of those titles would simply mean that I was one of a couple of thousand other private dicks, but they would sound better.

I didn't feel like a so-called private detective, of book and movie and radio and television fame, but I guess I was one, whether I felt like one or not. Maybe not a good one, with a crime laboratory in my library, if I had a library; just a back-alley operator trying to earn a few bucks without working too hard. I sometimes thought of rejoining one of the big agencies, but then I would lose my independence and it would be the clock-punching deal, and I didn't want that.

So I let Vivian Prosper call me a private detective, and I said, "I had a rough afternoon. Where are you?"

"At home. Why didn't you call me?"

"Give me time."

"Have you had dinner yet?"

"No," I said.

"Neither have I. Would you like to have it with me?"

"Of course. Where?"

"It doesn't matter. I want to see you. Linda still won't talk sense. Sergeant Navarre just left, and there are two policemen watching the house. I feel penned in. I want to get out."

"Come on over," I said. "I've got two steaks in the freezer. I'll start thawing them right away."

"Now, really," she said. "You mean in your apartment? Just the two of us?"

The coyness irritated me. "Well, I used to be a boy scout. I could build a fire down on the sidewalk and roast the steaks on sticks."

She laughed softly. "All right. How soon?"

"Now."

"The steaks won't thaw that quickly."

"All right," I said. "Make it an hour and a half. The steaks will be bloody and limp by then. I'll get some more sleep in the meantime." To hell with her.

"I like a drink before dinner."

"Make up your mind. If you come over now, you'll get a drink. What do you like?"

"Martinis, very dry."

"Dry it is," I said, hoping that I had gin and vermouth on hand.

She laughed again, a little nervously, I thought. "You make it sound very attractive."

"Attractive enough?" Suddenly I was remembering the feel of her body against me and the pressure of her lips.

"Very," she said. "Almost too attractive. Are you sure you want me? Really, I haven't been anywhere for so long, I—I won't know how to act."

"I'll teach you," I said, and I wondered if I should tell her that I had some etchings to show her.

"I want to talk to you about Linda." Her voice was suddenly crisp and cool.

"Of course," I said.

"Do you have anything to report?"

"A little."

"What?"

"I've got to get those steaks out," I told her. "I'll tell you when you get here."

"All right. A half hour?"

"Fine." I hung up.

I had time to get the steaks out, shave, put on a pair of cord slacks and a dark blue sport shirt, and mix a shaker of Martinis before my buzzer let loose.

She was wearing a soft gray dress, simple and severe, with a high modest neckline. Her tawny hair was combed back over her ears and tied with a dark blue ribbon. She seemed softer and younger than she had when I'd left her at noon. Her smile was almost shy.

"You look different," she said.

As I closed the door, I said, "How?"

"Just different. Nicer, somehow."

"I was just thinking the same about you," I told her.

She moved to the divan, sat down, and demurely smoothed the gray dress over her knees. I offered her a cigarette, but she shook her head. "How about that Martini?"

"Coming up." I went to the kitchen, got the shaker out of the refrigerator, dropped a couple of olives into two cocktail glasses, and carried it all into the living room.

"Oh," she said. "So you really have Martinis?"

"Of course."

"How nice."

I handed her a glass and her hand was steady as I filled it. She sipped, and said, "Marvelous. Where did you learn to make them that good?"

I said modestly, "It's one of my few accomplishments. I learned when I was in college."

She raised her brows. "Did they teach bartending at your college?"

"I worked in a bar at night to help with my tuition. The bartender who taught me was famous for his Martinis. He made them three parts gin to one part vermouth, just a dash of orange bitters. Stir gently and pour at the precise moment of ice dilution. Of course, I really should have a small sliver of lemon peel in them, but I'm fresh out of lemons, and—"

"Did you really go to college?" she broke in curiously.

"Do I seem too uncouth to be a college man?"

"No, no. You just didn't seem to be the—the type. What did you study?"

"Industrial engineering. But one year in an automobile plant cured me. I decided that life was too short to be constantly bucking departmental politics. Besides, the president's daughter was already married. So I quit."

"And became a private detective?"

"Please," I said. "I'm an investigator, a trouble-shooter. I try to help people—if they pay me. I don't detect, and I don't make as much money as an industrial engineer, but I'm my own boss."

She gazed around at my apartment. "You seem to do all right."

"Sure, for me. But what if I had a wife and four kids?"

She smiled up at me. "Just a family man at heart? Were you ever married?"

I shook my head.

"Would you like to be married?"

"I couldn't support a wife."

"You don't have to be a private de—an investigator always, do you?"

"Until something better comes along. And I haven't found it yet."

"Do you have any family?" she asked.

"My parents are dead, but I have a sister in Milwaukee. She's married to a lawyer, and they have two kids, a boy and a girl. The boy is in high school, and the girl is in the fourth grade. She's a Brownie in the Girl Scouts. And I have a brother, a doctor, who lives in New Jersey. He's a pediatrician, but he has no kids of his own. His wife is an invalid, and—" I broke off and grinned at her. "Do you want to hear family history?"

She gazed at me thoughtfully. "I'd like to," she said quietly.

"Not tonight." I refilled her glass, and mine, too, and sat down beside her. "Shall I put the steaks on?"

"Not yet. I'll have a cigarette now."

I lit one for her. She exhaled smoke at the ceiling and said, "What are we going to do about Linda?"

I said, "I found out a little this afternoon. Last night she was in a place called the Venice Café, with two men. One of them was the dead man in her car. Anyhow, I think so. The description checked. I don't know who the other man was."

"Spotwood," she said bitterly. "Arthur Spotwood, no doubt. The Venice Café? How did you know that she was there?"

"I saw a match cover in her car. I took a chance, and I hit."

"Oh, a clue?"

I winced again. "Please. It was just a hunch, and I was lucky. Did you telephone me there this afternoon?"

She turned her head quickly and her eyes were big and round. "Of course not. I never heard of the place until now. Why do you ask that?"

"Never mind," I said, remembering with a shudder the smell of the fish and the tartar sauce when my face hit the plate. My throat was still sore from the stomach pump. The two Martinis were getting to me, and realized that I hadn't eaten anything since the milk and toast in the afternoon. I thought hungrily of the steak, and I said, "Ready to eat now?"

She held out her glass. "May I have one more?"

As I poured for both of us I noted with dismay that the shaker was still half full. Another drink for me and wouldn't care if I never ate.

Her "one more" stretched into three more for her and two for me. That was plenty for both of us and I didn't make a move to refill the shaker. I didn't make a move to do anything, not even to broil the steaks. I just wanted to sit on the divan and listen to Vivian Prosper's low voice go on and on telling me about her life with her ex-husband, Allan Frederick Keeler, and her reasons for divorcing him.

"And then one afternoon," she said, "when I canceled a bridge date and came home unexpectedly, I walked into Linda's bedroom and found Allan in bed with her. That was the end. That's when I started divorce proceedings."

"Naturally," I said. "You couldn't have that. A hell of a thing." I was remembering with keen interest Linda's jealousy of her older sister. "And it wasn't very nice of Linda," I added.

"Oh, I don't blame her too much. Not really, I guess. She's just a kid yet, and a strange girl. She's wild and headstrong, and sometimes I think that she—she hates me. I've tried to take care of her, but for some reason she resents me. But she went too far. Allan was married to me, and I wouldn't stand for anything like that, not in my own house."

"Jerome's house," I corrected her.

"All right," she snapped. "My *home*, then. Are you listening to me?"

"Sure." I reached for the shaker, but remembered that it was empty. But she saw me reach, and said, "May have another drink?"

"Sure," I mumbled. "Sure thing." I got up stiffly, picked up the shaker, and carried it to the kitchen. I looked at the steaks, and I felt like eating one raw. I stirred a medium-sized batch of Martinis and went back to the living room. Vivian Prosper had kicked off her shoes and her nylon-clad feet were resting on the coffee table.

As I filled her glass, she said wistfully, "I don't think Linda cared for Allan—not really and truly. It was just something crazy to do, to get even with me for trying to discipline her. But she knows that I was only trying to help her and take care of her like Mother wanted. But I've failed, and she hates me." She sighed, and then she said, "But Allan shouldn't have been so weak, should he?"

"No," I agreed. "Very weak of him."

"You wouldn't do a thing like that, would you?"

"Not me. No, ma'am."

She smiled and patted my knee. "I know you wouldn't. You have—you have character. I learned that this morning."

I said, "If this Allan was such a heel, why did you marry him?"

She sighed and took a sip of her drink. "Have you ever been lonely?"

"Many times."

"Then you know what it is. After Mother died I was lonely and restless. Life didn't seem to have much point. Linda was still in high school and Jerome was busy with his own affairs—hunting, fishing, drinking, his women—you know? Then I met Allan at a party one night. I thought he was very handsome, in a sad poetic sort of way, and he was attentive to me. I liked it. Nobody had particularly bothered about me for a long time. Oh, I had the usual men around, but none of them interested me, and I was bored by all of them. But Allan was different, I thought—sort of artistic and sensitive and kind—and for a month or two I saw a lot of him. When he asked me to marry him, I accepted. We were happy for a while—I was, anyhow—and he continued with his work. He's a pharmacist, you know. But it wasn't satisfactory—his working, I mean. It interfered with our social engagements, and I persuaded him to drop it."

"Was it difficult to persuade him?" I asked.

"No," she said seriously. "Allan was very understanding, I must admit."

"So you and Allan lived the gay life on your money; until you caught him in bed with Linda?"

"Please don't be crude," she said. "I was bored with him anyhow. I was glad to get rid of him."

"Poor Allan," I sighed.

"Pooh," she said. "Pooh on Allan. A weakling, a—a—"

"A fortune-hunting bastard," I supplied for her. "A dumb yokel who had the world by the tail, and he killed the goose that laid the golden eggs."

"Are you calling me a goose, Mr. Brice?" She raised her eyebrows archly.

"No. It's just a corny mixed metaphor, and I'm sorry. Forget it. Look, I've got a couple of steaks out there ..."

"Do you think Allan has been seeing Linda?" she asked darkly. "I mean, lately? I know he saw her a few times shortly after the divorce. And he's a pharmacist, and he knows about drugs, and Linda was doped with morphine."

"To hell with Allan," I said.

"Good." She leaned against me. "Let's talk about us."

I filled her glass and mine, too, and I leaned back. To hell with the steaks, too. "Let's," I said.

"First, I want to tell you that I'm sorry for what happened this morning—about what I wanted to do."

"That's all right."

"But it wasn't all right. It was a wild idea, and very wrong of me. But I was thinking of protecting Linda. She was all I was thinking of."

"Sure," I said.

"Don't you believe me?"

I turned my head. Our noses were about six inches apart. Her eyes looked as big as swimming pools and there were tiny dancing lights in them. "Was that the only reason you were nice to me?" I asked. "Because you wanted me to help you?"

The swimming pools disappeared behind pale lids and her lashes were like a fringe of wet sand on her cheeks. "Of course," she whispered. "At first."

"Then what?"

"After you kissed me—then I'm afraid I wasn't thinking entirely of Linda. But I liked you even better when you refused to help me, no matter how I acted. I wanted desperately for you to do what I wanted, but I liked you better when you refused."

"I'm sorry about that," I said.

"Why?" she said quickly, and her eyes opened wide.

"Because," I said carefully, "if I had helped you to get rid of that dead man, you would have had to keep your promise to me."

"What promise? I don't remember any promise."

"All right," I said. "But if you *had* made a promise, would you have kept it?"

"No. Not a promise like that, no matter what I may have implied. I would have paid you, in money, but in—in no other way. It would have been too much like—like ..."

"Prostitution?"

"Yes. An ugly word, but that's how I would have felt about it."

"Then," I said, "in refusing, I was smarter than I thought. There wouldn't have been a pay-off."

She reclined beside me, her head resting against the back of the divan, her face turned toward me. Her eyes were big and thoughtful. "Don't talk like that," she said softly. "You're too bitter, too cynical. You don't have any illusions. Must there always be a pay-off?"

"Yes," I said, "in my book. It's what makes things tick."

She smiled faintly and I saw the slow throb of a vein in her throat. "No matter what happens to Linda," she said, "I'll always admire you for refusing me. I'm glad you refused me. If you hadn't, I would have felt nothing but contempt for you."

I placed my glass on the table and leaned back. "What do you feel now?" I asked her.

She didn't answer my question. "Would you refuse me again?" she asked.

"Refuse you what?"

"This," she whispered, and she placed a hand on my cheek and moved against me. Her lips were warm and soft and alive against mine and her arm slid up under my arms and across my shoulders. This was the back door to paradise, a paradise I hadn't earned, but it was here, now, waiting for me. I knew it, and she knew it; that was why she had come to see me. It was something between the two of us, something we both wanted, and nobody was being hurt. Her mouth clung to mine and her breasts pushed hard against me. I wondered fleetingly what had happened to her glass, and then out of the corner of my eye I saw it rolling across the rug.

Presently she moved her lips away and whispered against my ear. "I'm tired, Andy."

"All right," I said, and I stood up and grasped her hand. "Come on."

"Will you make me a drink first?"

"*Another* Martini?"

She shook her head and placed a finger beneath her chin. "I'm up to here with Martinis. Do you have any bourbon?"

"Sure," I said. Suddenly I leaned down and picked her up.

"You fool," she said, but she was laughing softly and happily as I carried her into the darkness of my bedroom and put her down.

"Bourbon coming up," I said, and I left her there.

As I moved through the apartment toward the kitchen I remembered the outer door and I checked it. It wasn't locked, and I was glad I had checked. I locked it and turned off all the lights except one dim lamp over my bookcase in the corner. The apartment took on a soft and cozy look, more pleasant than I ever remembered seeing it before, and I decided that it was probably due to Vivian Prosper's presence. I quickened my steps to the kitchen.

Ice in two tall glasses, two ounces of bonded bourbon, then soda, not too much. I put the steaks in the refrigerator, turned off the kitchen lights, and carried the glasses to the living room. It still looked soft and cozy, but the darkened door beyond beckoned to me. I paused a moment, sipping at my drink, gazing about. It had been a long time since I'd spent a complete evening in the three rooms I called home. But then, it'd been a long time since I'd had a visitor with the attractions of Vivian Prosper.

I moved to the bedroom door. The dim light behind me cast a faint yellowness over the floor, and through the screened window beyond I could see the dark glow of the tight sky. I couldn't see Vivian Prosper, and I had a sick feeling of panic, of paradise lost, and I stood in the doorway, holding the glasses and staring dumbly.

Then, on the floor, near the foot of my bed, just beyond the path of light, I saw a small gossamer mound of clothing—stockings, panties, bra, slip. Beside them was the gray dress, folded neatly. I took a quick breath and stepped into the room. I could see her then, very dimly, reclining against the headboard of the bed. Even in the semidarkness I knew that she was more beautiful than I ever could have imagined and I gazed at her almost in awe.

I moved slowly to her then and held out her glass. She took it from me, her fingers touching mine. I sat beside her, but I didn't touch her, and I found that I was trembling a little. We drank our drinks and talked in low hesitant tones, and the sound of the traffic in the street below died to an after-midnight whisper. Through the window we could see the night sky, and the stars began to fade a little. At last she handed me her empty glass.

"Another?" I asked.

She shook her head silently and stretched out with a contented sigh.

I carried the glasses out. When I returned to the darkened bedroom a cool night breeze caressed my body, and the curtains blew gently inward. Vivian Prosper stirred a little and flung out an arm in lazy invitation. I stretched out beside her, and she turned toward me. Her body was as soft and as cool as the night breeze.

In the gray dawn she awoke me. "I'd better go now," she whispered with her lips against my ear.

I pulled her to me. "No," I said.

Chapter Seven

At ten in the morning we had the steaks at last, with toast and orange juice. It was very pleasant sitting across the table in my sunlit kitchen having a second cup of coffee with Vivian Prosper. She had wrapped an old bathrobe of mine around her, and even without make-up she looked marvelous. The robe kept flopping open in front and she kept pulling it together. At last she said, "To hell with it," and she let it hang open.

"Good," I said, and we both laughed.

She washed the dishes while I showered, shaved, and dressed. When I left the bathroom and entered the bedroom, she too was dressed and ready to leave. She had combed her hair and applied make-up and she looked like what she was, an extraordinarily attractive rich woman groomed for the street. I had a quick feeling of pride in her, of possession.

"Leaving?" I said.

"I must. I've stayed too long now."

"Not long enough."

She smiled. "I'll be back."

"Promise?"

She nodded.

I stepped up to her and pulled her to me, but she wouldn't let me kiss her. "My lipstick," she said.

"You'll smear it." Her body was rigid beneath my hands. With Vivian Prosper there was a time and a place and a mood for everything.

I thought of something then, and I got her little .22 automatic from my coat pocket and handed it to her. She looked surprised. "Oh, I'd forgotten you had that." She took it carelessly, put it in her red leather purse, snapped the purse firmly shut, and moved past me. I followed her across the room and we stood by the door gazing at each other.

"Thank you," she said soberly.

I didn't say anything. What can a man say to a remark like that?

"I'll go out very quickly," she said, "and unobtrusively. Will I see you tonight?"

"Sure."

"Here? About six?"

"Fine," I said.

She smiled, slipped out, and quietly closed the door.

I made more coffee, lit a cigarette, and sat down at the kitchen table. I wanted to think a little, and plan the day's campaign. I had an office downtown, or rather a desk in a big room. I shared the room with two insurance salesmen, a young attorney just out of law school, a real-estate agent, and an elderly lady named Rosemary, whom we called Rosy. She conducted a mail-order business, selling a bottled green liquid known as Sta-Norm, which she described vaguely as beneficial for "female trouble." We all kidded her about it, but she sold gallons of the stuff, and maybe it was an effective elixir, for all I knew.

A desk in the room cost me thirty dollars a month, but I was rarely there. Most of the time I preferred to work from my apartment. It was easier to talk to people there than to compete with a buzz of conversation all around me dealing with twenty-pay life, executors and executrices, five rooms and a bath with a double garage, and "Why, sure, honey, Sta-Norm will fix you right up."

I decided where I would start my day's work and I went to the bedroom and put on a necktie and shirt. The illusive fragrance of Vivian Prosper still lingered and I began to anticipate our meeting in the evening. As I left the bedroom, the phone began to ring. I picked it up.

"Hello," she said. "How have you been?"

"Lonesome. Why don't you come over?"

She laughed. "What did you do—go back to bed?"

"No, but it's a good idea. I was just going to work."

"Listen, Andy. When I got home, Arthur Spotwood was waiting for me."

"Heavens," I said. "Did he know that you had been out all night?"

"Of course not." She laughed. "I told him that I'd been out doing the morning marketing. He's in the library now. I'm calling from the kitchen phone. He insists on seeing Linda. What should I do?"

"Let him see her."

"Are you sure it's all right? Those policemen are still camped outside. They know Arthur is here."

"What of it? Navarre probably has a tail on him."

"All right," she said. "Whatever you say. Don't forget tonight."

"I won't."

"Good-by, darling." She hung up.

That damn darling again. But now it sounded different. After last night I figured she had a right to call me darling. I even liked it a little. Nobody had called me that since I'd stopped seeing a redhead who sang in a South Side night club. The redhead had married the drummer in the band. The few girls I'd been with since had called me Andy, Andy dear, or honey, and one tall cool babe had called me Andrew.

My apartment buzzer let loose. I crossed to the door and opened it.

Jerome K. Pitt stood there, looking like an ad for a Miami Beach hotel. He was wearing a chocolate-colored Shetland jacket, a pale green shirt with the hand-stitched collar flared nicely over the lapels of the jacket, tan flannel slacks, green socks, and brown moccasins. He was freshly shaved and the rich odor of shaving lotion preceded him into the apartment. His heavy face looked blotched and bloated beneath the sunburn and there were delicate blue pouches beneath his eyes. I closed the door and he turned toward me exuding whisky fumes. The whisky smell mixed nicely with the shaving-lotion.

"Sit down, Mr. Pitt," I said politely. "Will you have a cup of coffee?"

His big body seemed to shudder. "Thank you, my boy," he said in his rich actor's voice, "but it's a little early in the day for coffee, isn't it?"

"I kind of like it for breakfast, but maybe I'm a little queer. Whisky?"

The whisky interested him very much. He relaxed and smiled at me. He had the most perfect set of upper and lower dentures I'd ever seen. They were made a little crooked, to look natural, and there was even a small gold filling in one of them. But the gums were just a little too pink. "Thank you, my boy," he said. "I don't mind if I do. Bourbon, please, if you have it. Just a small shot, about a tumblerful, with a little water on the side."

"Shall I just bring in the bottle?" I asked him.

His eyes brightened. "Will you have one too?"

I shook my head. "A little early in the day for me." I went to the kitchen. My liquor supply had taken a beating lately, but the bourbon bottle was still half full. I found a medium-sized highball glass, filled another glass with water and added a couple of ice cubes, and carried the glasses and the bottle into the living room.

I placed everything on the table before Jerome Pitt and told him to help himself.

He didn't hesitate and his hands trembled only a little as he filled a glass with whisky. I watched him, fascinated, as he swallowed a good third of it in one gulp. Then he shivered slightly as the whisky hit bottom. He took a sip of the water. "I needed that," he said huskily.

"A little hair of the dog?"

He smiled ruefully. "I'm afraid so, my boy. I've been rather upset about this nasty mess Linda is in, and I possibly consumed a mite too much last night." He smiled at me, man to man. "You know how it is."

"Sure," I said. At close range I rather liked Jerome K. Pitt. He reminded me of a football coach I once had in high school; they had the same thick build, blue eyes, heavy features like those of a reformed heavyweight, a little boy's snub nose, round chin, the same pinkish complexion. The coach's name, now that I was remembering, had been Pinky O'Roark. I tried to think of his real first name, but I couldn't. Even so, I could still remember Pinky slapping me on the rump at the half of the big game with Central High and urging me fiercely to "get in there and fight, Brice." I had played tackle, and on the first play of the second half a lard-hipped fullback had clipped me from behind and broken my leg. Pinky had come to the hospital to see me, and he'd had the same pathetic, half-apologetic look on his face that Jerome Pitt now had.

He looked at the remaining whisky in his glass and the whole story was in his eyes. Should he drink it all now, or string it out politely and make it last? He decided to make it last, and reluctantly his gaze left the glass, flicked over the bottle, and fell on me. "Have you found him yet?" he asked.

"Who?"

"The man who murdered that man in Linda's car?"

"No."

"But you're pretty certain to catch him?"

"I'm not at all sure, Mr. Pitt, and neither are the police. You can never be sure, but we're trying."

He leaned forward and his heavy face took on a just-between-us-men expression. "Confidentially," he said, "I'm not particularly concerned about the—the killing. For all I care, you can forget it and concentrate on opposing Vivian in her headstrong and selfish desire to keep Linda and Arthur Spotwood apart. The sooner Linda marries Arthur, the better everything will be." He slammed a fist into a palm with a soft smacking sound. "By gad, she's *got* to marry Arthur:" His three chins quivered.

He looked so earnest, so do-or-die, so pathetic, that I said, without thinking, "Mr. Pitt, were you ever a football coach?"

He turned his pale blue eyes upon me with a sad look of reproach. "Isn't that rather off the subject, young man?"

"Maybe. But you want the home team to win, don't you? And the home team is you and Vivian and Linda and me. What team are we playing? The cops?"

He said firmly, "The team we are playing is composed of one player—Vivian. And you omitted our most important star in your line-up—Arthur Spotwood."

"V. Prosper replaced by A. Spotwood," I murmured, "What's the signal?"

He smiled shyly. "You know, I played football once."

"In college?"

"No, no. I didn't go to college. I played for the Olive Street Junior High School. I was a second-string guard." He sighed heavily. "I had to quit school after the ninth grade."

"You seem to have done all right."

He looked at me. "I came up the hard way, young man."

"Rags to riches?"

He shook his head. His eyes were straining now to the whisky in his glass. He made up his mind and boldly reached out and picked it up and drank another third. As he sipped the water, he said, "Never any rags. Never, never the rags. Starve first, but always dress well." He waggled a stubby finger at me. "That is the secret of my success. There is no excuse for a man ever to be dirty or shabby. Soap and water are cheap. And keep your suits cleaned and pressed, your shoes heeled and shined, and your shirts starched. Even if you skip some meals. Appearances are what count, young man. Always remember that."

"Yes, sir."

"I was down to my last thirty-five cents when I met Edna," he said. "But my shoes were shined and I recall that I was wearing my best suit, a Scotch plaid with a subdued pattern, a fresh shirt, and a maroon knit tie. And I had a cornflower in my lapel. Not a carnation, mind you. That's too obvious. A cornflower is casual, devil-may-care, you know?"

"Yes, sir," I said. "Was Edna the mother of Vivian and Linda?"

"Yes," he said solemnly. "Edna, my one great love. May her sweet, generous soul rest in peace. She had just lost her husband when I met her. She was sitting by the lagoon in the park, dressed all in black. I happened by, wearing my Scotch plaid, and she looked so lonely and so lovely that I spoke to her. We talked, and she told me about her bereavement. I spent the thirty-five cents to buy bread to toss to the swans on the lagoon. It impressed her more than champagne cocktails, really. A month later we were married." He bowed his head. "Dear, sweet Edna," he said reverently.

I looked at my wrist watch. It was almost noon. I said, "Mr. Pitt, this is very pleasant, but I have an appointment shortly. Did you want to see me about something special?"

He looked up at me and his eyes were bleary with tears. "What?" he said blankly.

To hell with it, I thought. I lifted the bourbon bottle and took a swallow. It tasted terrible, and I damn near strangled. I put it back on the table and coughed violently. I was not a morning drinker, I could never be a morning drinker, and I might as well stop acting smart. I lit a cigarette, coughed on it too, and said bluntly, "I've got to leave. What do you have on your mind?"

"Money," he said sadly.

"Don't we all?" I snapped.

He looked up at me. "You seemed like a friendly young man," he said reproachfully. "But now you appear to be—uh—irritated. Have I offended you?"

"No, sir. It's just that I have things to do. Why did you come here?"

He tossed off the last third of the whisky in his glass and then eyed the bottle longingly. I decided that he'd had plenty, and I didn't say anything. He gazed at the bottle, rather pointedly, for maybe thirty seconds. I still didn't say anything. At last he raised his eyes, sighed, and said, "Don't you like money?"

"I love it."

"So do I, so do I," he said eagerly. "But it has always been my downfall. I love money so very much, but I can't hang onto it. I keep losing what I love. You know, the trouble is, I love the things money can buy. If I can't have them, I may as well be dead. That's the way I am. Edna knew this, and she was very generous with me. A wonderful, wonderful woman. Truly a jewel. She was the nicest and the most generous of all of them. I came to love her very much, really I did, and I tried to be a good husband, as good a husband as I can ever be. When Edna died I thought the world had ended for me." He paused, and his tongue flicked over his lips. Shyly he put his hand on the bottle and said, "May I, young man?"

"Go ahead—if you want to get falling-down drunk before noon."

He jerked his hand back as if a snake had bitten him, and he lowered his eyes and mumbled, "I know I drink too much. But it doesn't seem to matter anymore, with Edna gone...."

"Didn't she leave you pretty well fixed?"

He nodded silently, his head hanging down. "Yes, yes, she did. Of course she did. Better than I expected, better than I deserve. But it's all gone now, all down the drain. I've squandered it, I admit it. Lately I've been forced to go to Vivian for money. Edna's will left Vivian a tidy sum, and Linda will come into her share when she's eighteen, next month. But Vivian is the executrix, and she has the power to dole it out to her—until Linda is married, and then she gets it without any strings, all of it. The rest was mine, but now it's gone. Gone, gone ..."

"Where?" I asked. "And how much?"

He shook his head slowly back and forth. "A quarter of a million, all gone. Don't ask me where it all went. I—I don't know. Bad investments, a little gambling, a lot of liquor, a hunting trip to Africa, grouse shoots in Idaho, a horse that never finished in the money, memberships in my clubs, clothes, cars, boats. An apartment in Chicago for a close personal friend who needs my help."

I pricked up my ears. This was getting interesting. "A blonde friend?" I asked.

"No, no," he said angrily. "Why do people always think of a blonde in connection with an apartment? Corinne has dark brown hair, the color of chestnuts. And in some ways, with all due respect for the dead, Corinne understands me better than Edna ever did. For example, just to take one small example, Edna was always unreasonably old-fashioned about taking off her clothes before me. She'd send me out of the room, and she'd get in bed and pull the sheet up, just as if she was about to have a surgical operation. But Corinne, she understands me, the true me, and—" He broke off and stared up at me with drunken bewildered eyes. "Why am I telling you all this?"

"You started it," I said. "Tell me more about Corinne."

"You don't understand," he said stiffly. "Nobody ever understands. My feeling for Corinne was something apart from my life with Edna, something that would never hurt her."

"As long as she didn't get wise," I said.

He sighed in resignation. "You just don't understand," he said heavily. "Poor, poor Edna." He looked slyly at the bottle, but I was watching him, and he lowered his gaze to the floor.

I felt a little sorry for him. "Go ahead," I said. "Have a drink. And tell me what you came here for."

He looked again at the bottle, but his pride wouldn't let him touch it now. He stood up and moved slowly across the room and there was a certain shabby dignity in his manner. At the door he turned and faced me. He was as tall as I was, and maybe fifty pounds heavier. He said stiffly, "I merely came to remind you of your obligation to me."

I said curiously, "Why are you so anxious for Spotwood to marry Linda?"

He shifted his gaze to the wall behind me and cleared his throat. "Uh—Arthur is a fine, upstanding young man, and—"

"You said that before," I broke in wearily. "There are a lot of fine upstanding young men. Why Spotwood?"

He shot a furtive glance over his shoulder, as he had done the previous day in the hall of the Prosper home, as if he expected eavesdroppers to be lurking in my apartment. Then he leaned toward me and said in a hoarse whisper, "Can you keep a secret?"

I nodded.

"All right," he said. "Arthur Spotwood and I have a gentlemen's agreement. I am to do everything possible to persuade Linda to marry him. If I succeed, Arthur has agreed to share with me the money Linda will receive when she is married—the money to which Arthur will have access as Linda's legal husband." He paused and added in a firm ringing voice, "I don't want Linda to marry anyone but Arthur."

"Naturally," I agreed.

"By gad, she's got to marry Arthur. And soon. I am desperate. It's my only chance. My back is to the wall. Certain obligations …"

"Corinne?" I asked.

"Yes, yes," he said. "But—"

"Gambling debts?" I broke in.

"Yes, those, too. And—and other things. I do not wish to discuss them. Look here, young man. I have been very frank with you—too frank, I might add. I hope you will respect my confidences. How much money did I give you yesterday?"

"Two hundred dollars."

"All right, that's what I thought I gave you. Now, listen carefully. Are you listening?"

"Yes, sir."

"I repeat my offer of yesterday, with an additional incentive. If you will oppose Vivian in her jealous desire to keep Linda and Arthur apart, and bring Arthur and Linda together, and let the police handle the matter of the dead man, I will give you one thousand dollars more."

"Of Linda's money? When you get it?"

"That is correct. I am short of cash at present."

"O.K.," I said. What could I lose?

"Then we understand each other?"

"Perfectly."

He nodded gravely, cast a final longing glance at the bottle, turned, and went out, closing the door quietly behind him.

I carried the whisky and the glasses back to the kitchen and poured myself the last of the coffee. As I drank it, I thought wryly that I still had two jobs; one was to prevent Arthur Spotwood and Linda Prosper from getting married, if and when I could clear Linda of murder complications, and the other job was to do everything possible to bring Linda and Arthur to the marriage bed. An odd situation, but one with intriguing possibilities. The more I thought about it, the more I liked it.

I put on my hat and coat and went out. I didn't take a gun. Guns can get you into trouble.

Chapter Eight

The Apex Drugstore was an enormous sprawling super-emporium dispensing everything from drugs to television sets. I wandered between brightly lighted aisles dazzled by the gleaming array of toys, radios, shaving appliances, hardware, cutlery, surgical supplies, magazines, vitamins, cigarettes, auto accessories, cameras, pipes—tiers of glittering merchandise without end. Even books. At the cosmetic counter a slim little girl with a red, red mouth and obviously false breasts spoke to me in a voice as low and well modulated as any movie star's. "May I help you, sir?"

"I'd like to see Mr. Keeler."

"You wish to get a prescription filled?"

"No. I just want to see Mr. Keeler."

"Mr. Deegan is the pharmacist on duty now. He will be glad to take care of you."

"I don't want to see Mr. Deegan. I want to see Mr. Keeler."

"Mr. Keeler is not on duty," she said coldly. "He is off duty on Wednesdays and Thursdays. This is Thursday."

"Thank you, miss." I gazed about. There had to be telephone booths in this place, maybe an airline and railroad terminal, an auto salesroom, and a bus stop. I spotted the booths about a block away against a far wall, six of them in a gleaming glass-doored row.

I moved away from the girl. She turned disdainfully away to apply more redness to her red, red lips. Keeler's name and address was in the book, and I dialed his number. No answer. I waited for ten rings before I hung up. Then I went back out to my car and headed across town.

Allan Frederick Keeler lived in an apartment building way the hell and gone uptown, close to the lake. It was not a select neighborhood, but it wasn't a slum either. The building was of red brick and fairly new and stylishly called the Tarlton Arms. There was a tile-floored entrance, with a triple row of mailboxes along one wall. A closed door on my right said, "Office." A marble stairway with worn rubber mats on the steps wound up into darkness. Beyond the mailboxes was an automatic elevator with the door open. I checked Keeler's apartment number on his mailbox. It was on the third floor, number 10-C. I took the elevator up.

I didn't get any response to the buzzer beside 10-C. I rattled my knuckles on the door. Nothing happened, and I stood in the hall trying to decide whether to go down to my car and get a flat little curved strip of steel I kept in the glove compartment along with a flashlight, a coil of rope, two skeleton keys, and a street map of the city. I never used any of these items, but I was a private detective and I felt that I was expected to have them. While I was pondering the weighty problem of whether to jimmy or not to jimmy the door, an old man in gray overalls and a blue-and-white striped engineer's cap came around the corner of the hall. He was carrying an insecticide sprayer.

I stopped him. "Pardon me, sir, but do you have a key to this apartment?"

"I got keys to all of 'em," he said, and he gave the insect gun a squirt at two flies crawling on the wall. The flies buzzed frantically in circles and fell to the floor, wiggling feebly. The old guy chuckled happily. He smelled of oil and insecticide and chewing tobacco.

I said importantly, "Please unlock this door." I opened my wallet and gave him a quick look at my driver's license. "Fire Department, making an inspection."

"All that stuff's handled in the office downstairs," he said. He gave the sprayer another squirt at a lone fly on the ceiling. The fly zoomed wildly and nose-dived to the carpet. He chuckled in satisfaction. "That sure gets 'em. Zing, and they're done for."

I peeled off a five-dollar bill and folded it the long way so that he could see the big fat 5. He took it quickly and stuffed it in his overall pocket. "I go in with you," he said. He produced a ring of keys and unlocked Keeler's door. I followed him in.

It was just an ordinary apartment, not very neat or very clean. Thirty seconds was all I needed to walk through the whole layout—living room, small bedroom, bath, tiny kitchen. The outside kitchen door was standing open and I saw the black steel bars of a fire-escape landing. I closed the door and went back into the living room. Just ordinary furniture—chairs, a low coffee table littered with old magazines and newspapers, a few books with familiar best-selling titles on a shelf beside a small gas-burning fireplace. Dirty heaped ash trays were everywhere. A red-white-and-gray striped necktie lay across the arm of a greasy-looking divan, and beside the necktie was a crumpled embroidered woman's handkerchief. I didn't smell the hand-kerchief. I wouldn't have smelled it for fifty bucks, not even if I was sure of getting a whiff of sexy perfume.

There was a telephone on a small table in one corner. The table had a single drawer and the top was littered with unopened envelopes bearing the return addresses of clothing stores, gas stations, a book club, a credit jeweler, a life-insurance company. All of them had the obvious cold look of notices stating that remittance was past due. I stood by the table and gazed around the room. I felt frustrated. No blood on the floor, no ripped-up evidence of a frenzied search, no corpse in the bathtub, no suicide notes, no nothing. Just the untidy stale-smelling quarters of a man named Keeler who had once been married to Vivian Prosper.

The old guy who had let me in was standing by with his insect gun on the alert, but apparently there were no flies in Keeler's apartment. He didn't pay any attention to me until I opened the drawer of the table bearing the telephone and the notices of unpaid obligations.

"Hey," he said. "Looking for fire in a drawer is extry." Only he didn't say "fire"—he pronounced it "far."

"If I find a far," I told him, "I'll pay extry."

He looked hurt, but he didn't say anything further and he permitted me to rummage through the drawer. All I found were more unpaid bills, some canceled checks, and old checkbook stubs. The balances on the stubs ranged from a couple of hundred dollars to overdrawn. Apparently, since his divorce from Vivian Prosper, Allan Frederick Keeler did not have much financial security. As I closed the drawer, a pad by the telephone caught my eye. It was filled with scribbled numbers and addresses. One number was circled and was followed by two letters that I guessed to be someone's initials: "Un 4000 (S.L.)" I tore the page from the pad and put it in my pocket. Don't ask me why; I didn't

know then what good it would do, and it was just
something that I thought I should do, probably because the number was circled.

Behind me the old guy said nervously, "Hey, Chief,
let's go. There ain't no far in this apartment."

"Shush," I said. "I'm the far inspector here."

From the bedroom came a loud groan.

The old guy's breath was hot on the back of my
neck. "Wh—what was that?"

"Shut up," I hissed. It scared me too. A hell of a
thing, a groan from what I had thought was an empty
apartment. I moved slowly into the bedroom. That
was where it had seemed to come from. The old guy
was almost stepping on my heels. Then we heard it
again, fainter, from the far side of the bed.

"Hark!" the old guy whispered, his breath on my
neck.

I moved around the foot of the bed and peered
down. A man was lying on the floor between the bed
and a high chest of drawers. He was a slender man
with a thin yellow mustache and thin white face. A
long strand of blond hair lay against his high forehead.
There was a bruised spot above his left eyebrow, and
a little blood. He was wearing tan gabardine slacks,
brown-and-white saddle oxfords, yellow socks. From
the open collar of his white shirt the unknotted ends of
a green-dotted bow tie lay loose across his chest. As I
watched, he moved his legs feebly and his mouth
opened and closed without any sound.

Behind me the old guy gulped. I looked at him.
"Keeler?" I asked. "The man who lives here?"

He nodded, his Adam's apple bobbing.

I moved around the bed, leaned down, and grasped
Keeler by the shoulders. I motioned to the old guy to
get his feet, and between us we hoisted him to the bed.
He flung out wildly with his arms, began to mumble
thickly. I held his shoulders against the bed. "Take it
easy," I said.

He opened his eyes suddenly, stared dumbly at me. "Somebody slug you?" I asked him.

His eyes were blank, like the eyes of a man awakening from deep sleep. Then he closed his eyes, as if he wanted to shut out what he saw, as if he didn't believe it, as if I were a dream, or a nightmare, maybe.

The old guy was bug-eyed. "You want me to call the cops or something?" he asked me.

I shook my head. "I'll handle it. He's a friend of mine. Thanks for letting me in."

He hesitated, peering at me with weak gray eyes. He held the insect sprayer in the crook of his arm, like a rifle. Then he turned and left the bedroom. But in a second he poked his head around the edge of the door. "Say, Chief, I guess maybe I'd better tell 'em down in the office that the far inspector is up here."

I handed him a dollar. "I guess maybe you'd better not."

He gave me a tobacco-toothed grin, took the dollar, and went out, giggling to himself at his smartness. I followed him across the living room to the door and locked it behind him. When I returned to the bedroom the man on the bed had opened his eyes again. "Hi," I said cheerfully.

He pushed himself to a sitting position. "Who the hell are you?" he asked. He was delicately handsome, with dark brooding eyes. A woman would have called him poetic-looking, and I thought of Vivian's description of him. Sensitive was the word, maybe, or Byronic. To me he looked like a blond Poe mourning for his lost Lenore.

I said, "My name's Brice. The janitor let me in, when you didn't answer the bell. It looks like somebody slugged you. Did they?"

He put cautious fingers to his head, and then looked at the fingers. There was a little blood on them. He grimaced faintly, distastefully, and wiped his fingers on the bed covering. "I don't know, exactly," he said. "I—I had just got home and started to change my clothes. I heard a noise behind me, and before I could turn something hit me on the head, and that's the last I remember." He fingered his head again. "It hurts," he added.

It didn't look like a very bad bump to me, but maybe he was the bruise-easily type. But I didn't know—it wasn't my head. I said, "The back door was open. That's the way he came in."

His eyes narrowed slightly. "How did *you* get in here?"

"I told you. The janitor let me in."

He sighed. "Oh, yes. I guess I'm still a little groggy." He got up from the bed abruptly, moved to the tall dresser, picked up a wallet, and peered into it, his fingers moving. Then he said in a relieved voice, "Anyhow, he didn't get my money."

"I probably scared him away," I said.

He looked at me thoughtfully. Then he said, "I suppose I should extend my thanks."

I grinned at him. "I didn't slug you."

He didn't smile. "I'll have to take your word for that. Why did you want to see me? I mean, badly enough to gain entrance when I didn't answer the bell?"

"I'll make it short," I said. "Maybe you'd better sit down."

"I'll stand," he said coldly. "Go on."

I didn't beat around the bush. "Linda Prosper came home yesterday morning with a dead man in her car. She was drunk, and she'd been doped—a big dose of morphine. I know you were once married to her sister, Vivian, and I wanted to ask you a few questions."

He sat down after all, quite suddenly, and he pulled a thin graceful hand down over his thin pale face. "Now, wait a minute. I don't get it. A dead man in Linda's car? Linda Prosper? Is that what you said?"

I nodded.

"Are you a policeman?"

"No. A detective, private. I'm working for Vivian."

"Why?" Now he really looked bewildered.

I said patiently, "Vivian is worried about Linda. The man in Linda's car didn't die of a heart attack. He was murdered, stabbed to death. And Linda won't talk. She refuses to tell us anything about her doings the night before last. The police are naturally interested in her, and they have a guard on the house. Vivian hired me to try to find out the facts—who the dead man is, what happened all about it, and clear Linda— if it's possible to clear her. Right now she's in it up to her neck. The cops won't fool around with her very long. The only reason they haven't got tough is because all they have so far is suspicion of implication in or knowledge of murder. They could take her to the poky as a material witness, but I suspect that they're moving slow because of her tender age, the peculiar circumstances, and her physical condition due to the dope. Right now they're playing kind of a waiting game, but the game is about to break up. Now do you get it?"

"Yes," he sighed. "I guess so. But I didn't see anything in the papers."

"The officer in charge is keeping it quiet, but it may break any time."

He shook his head. "It sounds like a tough deal for Linda, but she's a girl who has to learn the hard way. What do you want with me?"

"You were once connected with the family, and I thought that maybe you could give me a line on some of Linda's friends. Vivian, apparently, has been unable to keep track of her." I described the man found in Linda's car. "Does he sound like anyone you know, or know of?"

"No," he said. "I'm afraid I can't be of much help. Linda is a cute kid, but she was pretty wild, when I last saw her. She ran around with different boys—and men—and in different crowds. But there was never anyone in particular, and I didn't pay much attention. I know that Vivian worried a lot about her, but, as you say, she couldn't keep track of her doings and her friends. She was in several unsavory situations while I was married to Vivian, but coming home with a corpse in her car ..." He shook his head. "Well, that's a new one."

"Do you know a man named Arthur Spotwood?" I asked him.

"Look," he said, "this is all too fast for me. I get knocked cold in my own bedroom and wake up with a strange guy asking me questions about a dead man in my ex-sister-in-law's car. I've tried to talk intelligently, but my head hurts and I don't feel too good. Spotwood, did you say?"

"Yes. Arthur."

"Never heard of him. Who is he?"

"One of Linda's current boy friends. He wants to marry her the worst kind of way. He claims he had dinner with her last night, but that he left her right afterward. I haven't bothered him yet, because the police will get to him pretty quickly. They'll probably get to you, too. I don't know. My coming here was just a shot in the dark, something the cops may not think of right away. I don't like to follow them around—it's duplication of work. Do you have any idea who could have been snooping around your apartment and slugged you?"

"Why should I?" he said. "You were snooping around—you thought I wasn't home. Maybe you slugged me." He gave me a grin, but there wasn't much mirth in it.

"We've gone over that," I said. "I'm trying to keep a jump ahead of the police. They're sure as hell going to book Linda, and soon, unless I can stir up something to change their minds. I'd appreciate anything you can tell me, anything at all."

"Like what?"

"Like the reason Vivian divorced you." I had finally said it. It was the reason I'd come to see Allan Frederick Keeler, the only reason. I watched him carefully.

His pale face took on a faint pink tinge beneath the delicate skin. The color made him appear more virile, not quite so poetic-looking. I liked him better with a little color in his face. The spot of blood on his high forehead didn't look quite so red. He ran a finger across his silky mustache and said in carefully controlled tones, "Listen, you damned son-of-a-bitch, how would you like to go to hell?"

"Now, now," I chided, "let's not spoil it. Do you want me to tell you why she divorced you?"

"I'd love it," he said coolly.

"Vivian told me that she caught you in bed with Linda."

"That's right," he said. "If you knew, why did you ask me?"

My estimation of Allan Frederick Keeler zoomed approximately three notches. No hedging, no hot righteous denials. We're all human, ain't we?

"How was it?" I asked him.

"Nice," he said. "Very nice. And since our conversation seems to have degenerated into locker-room gossip, how is *your* sex life?"

"Adequate," I said. "Quite adequate at present." I was thinking of Vivian Prosper. "Did you have to coax her?"

"Do you know Linda?"

"Only slightly."

"Then I'd better tell you that I didn't have to coax her. She coaxed me. Does that sound like boasting?"

"No," I said, remembering this time the other Prosper sister, the younger one named Linda, who had nibbled at my ear with her pajama top falling off her. "No, it doesn't sound like boasting at all."

"Honest to God," he said, "I couldn't beat her off with a club. No kidding. She's wild. And besides, she'd been working on me for a long time, and a man can stand just so much. It was very unfortunate that Vivian discovered us, but Linda was delighted. She hates Vivian, you know."

"I don't think so," I said. "She's jealous, and maybe she has a 'get even' complex generated by concentrated maternal affection upon Vivian."

"So you're a psychologist, too?" he said mockingly. He paused, and then said soberly, "But you've probably hit it. I never thought about Linda in that way before."

I said, "And so Vivian divorced you, and you had to go back to work?"

He nodded gloomily.

"Too bad," I said. "All that Prosper money. But didn't you try to defend yourself, maybe tell Vivian that Linda provoked you beyond the limits of a man's natural human behavior?"

"Hell, no," he said bitterly. "What good would that have done? It wouldn't have excused me, and besides, Linda swore that I seduced her."

Another notch for Allan Frederick Keeler. A tough deal for him. Judging from what I'd seen of Linda's actions, I couldn't blame him too much. It could happen to anybody; in fact, it had almost happened to me. But then, I wasn't married. I'm old-fashioned enough to believe that once people get married, they should stay on their own side of the fence, no matter how much greener the grass looks on the other side. But married men made of sterner stuff than Allan Keeler had succumbed to the wiles of females with less attraction than Linda Prosper. It happened every day, every hour, every minute, I guess.

I said, "And so you left the Prosper household and haven't had anything to do with any of them since?"

"That's right."

"You haven't—uh—seen Linda? I mean, since? You had a nice memory of her. Didn't you want to freshen the memory a bit, even after the way she'd treated you?"

"Of course," he said. "Wouldn't you?"

I admitted that I probably would, and asked, "But she refused to see you?"

"Yes. I called her a couple of times, but she brushed me off. She was through with me." He gave me a crooked grin. "That little gal is dynamite, jail bait. I'm well out of it, and I intend to stay out."

"O.K. Now would you mind telling me where you were the night before last?"

"Still the cop, huh?"

"It's just a routine question."

"I went to a movie," he said. "I came home around midnight and went to bed."

"What movie?"

"The Lakeview Drive-In. The feature was Toni Lord in 'The Devil's Price.'"

"Good," I said. "Now, can you prove that you were home at midnight, and that you stayed home?"

"No. I don't have to prove it. But it's true."

"You don't have to prove it to me, but the cops will want to know, when they get around to you."

"I'm not worried," he said, smiling. He had strong white teeth, very bright and clean-looking.

I moved to the door. "Well, thanks."

He got up from the bed and followed me. "I'm sorry I can't be more help," he said, "but if I get any ideas, I'll let you know. I suppose you're in the phone book?"

"Brice. Andrew H."

He touched the bruised spot on his head. "Do you think I should tell the police about this?"

I shrugged. "If you want to. I'm afraid it won't do any good. But I advise you to keep your doors locked."

"A locked door didn't keep you from coming in," he said, smiling.

"Still harping on that, huh? Listen, I could do a better job of slugging you with my head in a burlap bag and my hands tied. He barely nicked you. You're lucky."

"No offense," he said. "Are you married?"

"Not yet. Why?"

"I know a few nice girls. Some evening when you aren't busy, give me a ring and we'll have a time. Most of my friends are married, and I get tired of single dates. I know a place up along the lake where they serve the biggest highballs and steaks in town, and the music is usually good. We'll make a double date of it."

I was touched. I hadn't heard the expression "double date" since my high-school days. "Why, thanks. I may do that."

"Fine," he said, smiling. "Give Vivian my love."

"What about Linda?"

"Give her my love, too."

"Right," I said.

I left him standing in the middle of the room smiling at me.

Chapter Nine

It was two o'clock in the afternoon and the city was bustling with midweek activity. The sun was hot, but a soft breeze blew in off the lake. Sparrows fluttered and chirped and pecked in the gutters and pigeons wheeled against the sky. Cars and busses and trucks moved along the street, and briskly walking people jammed the sidewalks. An old scabrous drunk with the neck of a wine bottle protruding from his shabby and sagging coat pocket shuffled past me, muttering obscenities to himself. A young mother and a blonde little girl with pigtails tied with red ribbons stood in front of a toyshop window. Men with briefcases hurried by, looking important. Half-grown kids shouted and hooted and ran between and around the pedestrians. An overpainted girl in a red silk blouse slowed her steps and gave me the familiar age-old glance in an attempt to drum up some afternoon business, but I shook my head at her cheerfully.

It was a normal summer afternoon in the city, and I felt normal and reasonably happy. I had work to do, two clients, a two-hundred-dollar advance with the prospects of more in the offing. My little talk with Allan Frederick Keeler had netted me nothing, but it had been a start and the day was young.

The breakfast steak had become a pleasant memory, and so I had two hot ham sandwiches with lettuce and tomato and two glasses of milk at a place I knew called Rostand's. Then I drove back across town to the far fringes where the cornfields merged with the four-lane highways and parked on the cinders behind the Venice Café.

The brunette waitress was wiping the top of the table in the end booth. There were only five people at the bar, an engrossed middle-aged couple and three lone men, and the jukebox was silent. The tables around the edge of the small dance floor were unoccupied, and Pablo, the bartender, was at the end of the bar stacking empty bottles in a big cardboard box. From the kitchen dishes rattled and the air-conditioning hummed monotonously. The whole place seemed to be settling into an afternoon lull.

I sat down at the booth where the brunette was slowly pushing a towel around. The paint on her fingernails was still chipped. I ordered coffee and she said, "Yes, sir, cream?" mechanically, and I said, "Black." The towel stopped moving and she looked at me for the first time.

"Hello," I said. If she'd lost thirty pounds and taken off most of that make-up she would have been rather pretty.

She smiled, showing good teeth. "No Manhattan today?"

So she remembered me. That was fine. "I guess I'm allergic to Manhattans."

"Boy, was you sick," she said.

I shuddered. "Don't remind me. I wanted to see you yesterday before I left, but I guess you had gone."

"I quit around three, after I get the tables wiped." She glanced at the clock behind the bar. "I'm almost finished now." She hesitated, and there was a look, a something, in her eyes. "Black coffee, did you say?"

"Forget the coffee. Can you talk a minute?"

She shot a glance toward the bar. "Well, I don't know. Guido's gone, but Pablo, he thinks he's the boss—when Guido's away, I mean. We ain't supposed to talk to customers."

"All right. Bring the coffee, finish your work, and I'll take you home. My car's in back—a black Ford."

"You might ask me first," she said coyly.

"May I have the pleasure of taking you home?" I didn't see any rings on her fingers and I took a chance on there being no husbands in the offing.

She moved the towel in a slow circle on the tabletop. "What did you have in mind?" she asked in a low voice. "I'm off the rest of the day."

"Just fun," I said. "A few drinks, maybe; some talk."

"More questions, like you started to ask me yesterday before you passed out?"

"Maybe."

"Nothing doing. I told you all I know."

I got another five-dollar bill from my pocket and laid it on the table. "You might remember some more," I said.

She started to reach for the money, and then withdrew her hand. "No," she said. "You paid me enough last night. But them drinks would be nice." She glanced over her shoulder, saw that Pablo was glaring at her, and added hurriedly, "I'll bring some coffee. Drink it and wait in your car. I'll finish up and come out." She moved back toward the kitchen.

Pablo resumed his bottle-dumping, and I lit a cigarette. The brunette came back with the coffee, wrote me a check for ten cents, said loudly, "Thank you, sir," and moved away to wipe the tables by the dance floor.

The middle-aged couple finished whatever they were drinking and stumbled out, giggling softly. The three men remaining at the bar sat motionless, and I wondered how long they had been there. I sipped at the coffee. In about five minutes the brunette finished the tables and disappeared through the kitchen door. I finished the coffee, laid a dime on the bar, and went out to my car.

In a couple of minutes the brunette came out of a back door, looked around, and came over to my Ford. I leaned over and opened the door for her. She was still wearing the white uniform and she carried a shabby-looking brown suede purse. "Golly," she said, "but I'm sick of that dump."

"Hard day?"

"They're all hard when you work for Guido. Say, would you get going, please? Old Pablo will stick his head out the door in a minute and squeal to Guido that I'm knocking off early to date the customers."

I started the Ford and eased it out to the highway. "Where to?" Even with the windows open, the brunette's heavy perfume was strong.

"Well," she said, "you mentioned a drink."

"At your place?"

"Naw. Nothing there but a half-bottle of fig wine. How about stopping at O'Brian's? It's just up the road."

"All right," I said, and I drove to O'Brian's.

It was almost an exact copy of the Venice Café, except that it didn't have air-conditioning. The brunette drank two double shots of rye with beer chasers while I was finishing one Scotch and soda. I tried to talk to her, but she wouldn't answer me and concentrated on the rye. Nobody paid any attention to us. When she'd finished her second drink there was a shine in her eyes and she smiled at me. "I feel better now," she said. "That dump sure gets me down."

"What's your name?"

"Blanche."

"Blanche what?"

"Never mind. Just Blanche. What's yours?"

"Andy."

She crossed a hand in front of her face, palm out. "Hi, Andy. How about another drink?"

"All right. But let's have it someplace else—where we can talk."

"You wanna *talk?*"

"A little."

"What about?"

"Those people I asked you about yesterday—the girl and the two men."

"Oh, *them.* Why? Is the dame your wife or something?"

"I told you I wasn't married."

"And I suppose that makes it true?" she said mockingly. "O.K. She's your girl friend, and she's cheating on you. Is that it?"

"Yeah. That's it."

She laughed loudly and banged her hand on the table. "That's good. And now you're out with me and cheating on *her.*"

An elderly man at a nearby table looked up from bowl of crackers and milk and gave us an annoyed stare. "Let's go," I said, and I stood up. I left some money on the table, grasped her arm, and pulled her to the door. She resisted at first, but by the time we reached my car she was pushing her body against my hip. It was one of those rare times when I wished I was in some other type of profession. As I drove away, she snuggled up against me, but I kept both hands on the wheel.

"Describe them again to me," I asked her. "The girl and the two men."

Her hand crept to my knee and stayed there, the fingers exerting a slight pressure. "I'll tell you what," she said, her voice a little thick. "You get a bottle of rye, and we'll go to my place, and I'll tell you all you want to know. I even know one of the men's name." She laughed up at me. "Wouldn't you like to know that?"

My hands tightened on the wheel. "How do you know his name?"

"That girl—Linda—called him by name. She was mad at him, and I heard her say, 'Listen, so-and-so, you dirty son-of-a-bitch.' That's what she said. Vulgar, wasn't she?"

"Skip the so-and-so. What did she call him?"

"Promise you'll get the rye? A fifth, not a lousy pint?"

"I promise."

"She called him Steve. That's all. But once she called the other guy by his full name, and I know what it is. *He's* the one you've got to worry about. She kissed him twice, while they was in the booth, but she just cussed the other guy. You don't have to worry about *him*."

"That's good," I said. "Who was one she kissed?"

"Wouldn't you like to know?" she said teasingly.

"You promised me," I said reproachfully, keeping my voice calm.

"I ain't seen that fifth of rye yet."

"Where do you live?"

"Getting anxious, honey? Turn right at the next street."

We were approaching the outskirts of the city, a smoke-blackened section of factories, coal yards, and rows of drab houses. I turned right at the next street and saw that it was bordered by small dingy stores with run-down houses between them. There wasn't any grass on the narrow boulevards and the street was bumpy and littered with tin cans and broken bottles. At the far end the houses and the stores thinned out and there were stretches of weedy vacant lots before the street dipped again to the valley and the factories and the railroad tracks below. Here, on a knoll, surrounded by a few scraggly trees, stood a big frame house with a long front porch and many gables, shutters, and fragile-looking balconies. I decided that it had been built by one of the early steel tycoons and had gradually been surrounded and isolated by the factories and the workers' shacks. A sign stuck into the hard clay of the front yard said: "Furnished Rooms and Apartments By Day or Week."

The brunette pointed at the house. "Stop there. That's where I live."

I stopped the Ford beneath the meager branches of a dying maple tree and went through the motions of hunting for a cigarette in order to get the brunette to move a little away from me. But she wouldn't move, and I gave up, feeling a kind of rage flow through me. She knew I wanted to know, and she had told me part of it. Linda Prosper had been in the Venice Café with two men. One of them, the one who was now dead, was named Steve. The other one, the one she had kissed, was—who? If I knew his name I could move fast, and Navarre could move fast. The brunette named Blanche knew his name, and all I had to do was to get her to tell me. I suppressed the feeling of rage, of frustration, and I placed an arm around the brunette's plump shoulders and drew her to me. The scent of her was almost overpowering.

She rubbed a full rounded calf against my leg laughed softly. "You're *really* anxious, ain't you?"

"You bet," I said.

"We don't have that rye yet," she reminded me.

I turned on the ignition and reached for the star button. "Let's go get it."

She rubbed my arm. "Listen, honey. I've got an idea. Let's make a real party of it. I'll go up and get the apartment straightened up a little—I didn't have time to make the bed this morning—and you go get some hamburger and some bread and potato chips and pickles and stuff, and the rye. Would you bring some beer, too? I like a beer rinse, don't you?"

"Sure. I like it fine."

She grasped my chin and shook my head. "Don't look so sad, silly. That skinny little Linda ain't worth worrying about. I'll show you, and you'll forget all about her. And if you really want to know, I'll tell you the name of the other guy."

"Tell me now," I said, with a last desperate hope.

She laughed deep in her throat. "I will, honey. Don't worry." She opened the door and started to get out. Then she paused and said, "Honey, you've been so nice and all, I almost forgot. Friends is friends, but I got a living to make. It'll cost you five bucks for a quickie, and fifteen bucks for an all-night job. But since you're buying the rye and the stuff, I'll make it ten. O.K.?"

"Swell," I said. "Cheap enough. A bargain."

"Oh, *you*," she said, wrinkling her nose. "You're cute. Hurry, now. My apartment is upstairs, at the back. I'll leave the door open a little." She got up and stood on the rutted bare earth of what had once been a green lawn.

"I wish you'd tell me—" I began, but my voice was just a lonely wail in the wilderness.

She reached out and patted my cheek. "I will,
honey. Don't you worry. I'll tell you that guy's name,
and some more stuff, too. I heard a lot they was talking
about, and you'll get a kick out of it. That Linda has
been in the place a lot, but it was the first time she
came in with those two guys. You just get the hamburger and the whisky and stuff, and we'll have a few
drinks, and I'll fry the hamburger and tell you all about
it, anything you want to know."

"All right," I sighed, and I started the motor.

As I pulled away, she called after me, "Better bring
a pound of butter and a bottle of ketchup. I just remembered I'm outa butter and ketchup."

"A pound of butter and a bottle of ketchup," I muttered to myself as I drove down the narrow cluttered
street.

It took me about fifteen minutes to find a delicates-
sen. Like any subdued husband with instructions from
his wife, I bought a pound of hamburger, a loaf of
bread, a small jar of pickles, a bag of potato chips, six
bottles of cold beer, a pound of butter, and a bottle of
ketchup. Then I drove ten blocks to the nearest state
liquor store. I don't like rye, but I bought a bottle of
the best they had, and made a mental note to include
everything on my expense account to Vivian Prosper.
It was almost four o'clock in the afternoon when I
stopped once more beneath the sickly branches of the
dying maple tree before the house where lived the brunette named Blanche.

I locked the Ford, and carrying my big paper bag
of provisions I went up a cracked walk to a sagging
porch. The front door was standing open and there
wasn't any screen. A swarm of flies buzzed around a
collection of unwashed milk bottles by the door, and a
child's broken wagon, rusty and battered, tilted on
three wheels at the far end of the porch. On the porch
railing three empty beer cans drew more flies. I peered
into a big gloomy hallway. Closed doors stretched

back into darkness. From somewhere came a baby's cry and a woman's shrill voice. I went up the uncarpeted stairway on worn and splintered wooden steps. At the top there was another hall with more closed doors and the stale smell of cooking and dead cigars and dead air. A radio blared from behind one of the doors.

I moved along the hall toward the rear of the house. She had said her door would be open, but all of the doors were closed, even the last one, where I had guessed her place to be. I turned the knob and the door swung inward. I knew I had guessed right, because I saw her worn brown suede purse on a chair. I pushed the door open all the way.

The brunette named Blanche was on the bed. She was on her back, her legs spread wide, her arms at her sides. She hadn't had time to change her uniform. It was almost a solid red from her waist up. Her mouth was open and her eyes were open, and blood still seeped from the stab wounds in and around her left breast. She hadn't been dead very long, but she was as dead as she would ever be.

I hated it, because she had died because of me, and because now she couldn't tell me the name of the other man with Linda Prosper, the man who had stayed alive while the man called Steve had ended up a corpse in Linda's car. I was sorry that she was dead. I am always sorry to see anyone dead, even my enemies. But there was one bright spot: It was no longer necessary for me to participate in the hamburger and rye whisky party, with beer chasers, at the reduced rate of ten dollars for the all-night job.

Chapter Ten

I didn't spend much time in the pitiful little space that the brunette named Blanche had called her "apartment." The bed was at one end of the small room, with a table, a lamp, and a couple of chairs at the other. A closet had been converted into a kitchen nook, and in it there was a small gas burner, a battered ice chest, and a tiny sink with a single water tap. I figured the bath, if there was a bath, was down the hall. A meager supply of clothing hung on hooks behind a suspended sheet in a corner. Everything was clean and tidy.

I opened the worn suede purse. A green imitation leather wallet contained two one-dollar bills, eighty-nine cents in change, and a Social Security card bearing the name of Blanche Dorinda Swickert. The purse also contained a fresh package of cigarettes, matches, a soiled handkerchief, three sticks of peppermint chewing gum, and a letter still in its torn-open envelope. It was postmarked at East Branch, Michigan, and the date was a month old. I took out the single ruled sheet and glanced at the wavering penciled words: "Dear Daughter, I wish you would come home. Your pa had a stroke a week ago Wednesday. He is in bed night and day and can't move. I have to feed him. Your brother Donald was drafted. He is in a camp in new jersey. Loretta has a Baby Boy. You would think Ralph would be happy and proud but he just gets drunk. It is terrible. Your pa is a awful care. I need you...."

I stopped reading, carefully placed the letter back in the envelope, and closed the purse. I left then, without looking again at what was on the bed, and quietly closed the door. I took the bag of groceries and the fifth of rye whisky. Blanche Dorinda Swickert wouldn't need them now. At a drugstore booth I called the nearest precinct station. It wasn't necessary, but I hated to think of Blanche Dorinda Swickert lying in a small closed room for maybe a couple of days during a hot week in August. I gave the name and address to the cop who answered, and hung up. I left right away, because I knew they'd try to trace the call, and I didn't want to be bothered with a lot of questions. Not now. There were things I wanted to do before the sun went down, and the day was waning. I could explain to Navarre later.

I drove clear to the lake shore before I stopped and hunted up a phone booth in a bus terminal. When I was inside with the door closed I took from my pocket the page I'd torn from the pad in Allan Frederick Keeler's apartment with the notation "Un 4000 (S.L.)." I dialed University 4000. I didn't have any particular reason—it was just one of those things you do when you've been in the business a long time. It was the last number written on Keeler's telephone pad, and either it meant something or it didn't. Maybe he wrote it, and maybe somebody else did. Maybe one of his girl friends, or the person who sneaked into his place and slugged him. The only way to make any progress was to call the number and then try to decide if the "S.L." written after it was somebody's initials, a brand of gin, or perhaps just a telephone-pad doodle.

A crisp female voice answered. "Good afternoon. Midstate University,"

That stopped me. From a fly-buzzing rat trap of a house to one of the biggest colleges in the Midwest. I couldn't think of a thing to say.

The female said impatiently, "Hello. This is Midstate University."

I found my voice. "Good afternoon, miss. Would you happen to know a Mr. Allan Frederick Keeler?"

"One moment, please. I'll connect you with the registrar's office."

There was a click and then another female voice said, "Registrar's office, good afternoon."

I repeated my question and the voice said, "Is he a student here?"

"Do you have a night school?"

"Yes, but—"

"I'll be over," I said, and I hung up. I went out to the street and walked to where I'd parked my car. It was a wild-goose chase maybe, but it was better than answering questions about how I found a dead brunette named Blanche Dorinda Swickert.

Midstate University was on the southern edge of town, still within the city limits, but in a quiet backwater away from the roar of traffic. There was a lot of green grass, tall old trees, winding paths, and the wall of a stadium looming above the chapel spire. I drove slowly around the campus until I came to a massive stone structure with "Administration Building" cut into a marble slab over the entrance. I parked my car at the edge of the drive and walked up six wide stone steps under the arch of the doorway.

It had been a long time since I'd been inside the cloistered halls of learning. There were wide cool corridors, frosted glass doors, and I smelled the odor of soap and stone and books. It carried me back more years than I cared to remember. The registrar's office was on the third door on my right. I went in.

A redhead with nice legs and a sprinkling of freckles was sitting behind a desk with an open front. She was wearing a white nylon blouse that revealed her slip and bra straps, a black linen skirt, and stubby red highheeled shoes with ankle straps. Behind her, facing the windows, was a bigger desk cluttered with papers. Two walls of the room were lined with gray steel filing cabinets. A glass-doored bookcase held six shelves of fat books with gilt dull-looking titles. The redhead looked up at me through a pair of glasses with greentinted frames. The rims were shaped like curved arrow heads with the points joining at the bridge of her nose.

I took off my hat. "Good afternoon." I glanced at her left hand, saw no rings, and added, "Miss."

She removed the glasses and laid them on the desk. Her eyes almost perfectly matched the green frames. "Good afternoon," she said coolly.

"Is the registrar in?"

"Not at present. I'm Miss Hart, his assistant. Can I help you?"

"Well—" I began.

"I know," she broke in. "You telephoned. I remember your voice. You asked about a person named Keeler, and then you hung up on me."

"You have a good ear for voices," I said.

She smiled faintly, her gaze going over my clothes, my shirt, my tie, and ending on my hair. I remembered that I needed a haircut. "I checked the student list," she said. "We have a George Washington Keeler in the School of Agriculture. He's a senior."

"Just forget about Keeler," I told her. "How about someone with the initials S.L.? Who could that be—at this telephone number?"

She put her glasses back on and looked me over some more. She was cagey. She wasn't answering foolish questions for every Tom, Dick, and Harry who walked into her office.

"Why?" she asked crisply.

"It'll be easy," I said. "Just check the L's on your list of students and find one whose first name begins with S." I remembered what the brunette had told me about Linda Prosper calling one of the men Steve, and I added, "Steve might be his first name."

"Really," she said, "this is very irregular. Don't you know the person's full name?"

"No, miss," I said patiently. "If you will let me see the list I will be glad to—"

"I know," she said with an edge to her voice. "You're a private eye tracking down a clue to a murder."

"Please. Don't be melodramatic."

"Well," she said, "if you're a bill collector, you'll have to see Mr. Jork, in the Personnel Building."

I sighed, took out my wallet, and showed her the photostat of my license. It was a last resort, and I hated to do it, but I didn't want to spend what was left of the day sparring with Miss Hart, pretty as she was.

She took one look and gasped, "Oh, my goodness! Don't tell me! You really *are* a detective?"

I nodded and wondered if I should start talking out of the side of my mouth.

"Like in the movies and books?" she breathed.

"No, miss, but it happens to be the way I make a living. Now, if you will please just check your list of students ..."

She removed her glasses again. Her eyes were friendly now. "Why didn't you tell me in the first place? My goodness, but I think this is interesting. A real live private detective. I never met one before. Do you carry a gun in a shoulder holster?"

"No, miss. Now—"

"Do you drink double shots of bourbon at every whip-stitch, and get all beat up, and wounded in the shoulder? Why do they always get shot in the shoulder? Do sexy blondes keep making passes at you, and are you always fighting with the police because you withhold important evidence, and they threaten to take away your license, only all along the police are dumb? But in the end you corner the killer, and he confesses, and then tries to get away, and you are forced to kill him, and—"

"My God, no!" I almost shouted. "Please. Just—"

"I just love whodunits," she panted. "I've got stacks and stacks of them at home. I just read a swell one last night called 'Perchance to Kill'. The murderer was a student of Shakespeare, and he was always reciting passages from Hamlet—you know, like 'To die, to sleep, perchance to dream?' Well, the main clue was something from Hamlet, and the detective pinned it on the Shakespeare student by changing the word 'dream' to 'kill'. Perchance to *kill*. Get it?"

"No," I snarled. "It sounds dumb to me. But—"

"And the beautiful blonde babe," she babbled on, "the wife of the dead man, falls for the detective, and absolutely *throws* herself at him, but he refuses her advances, in a nice way, of course, because he is being true to Lorna, his cute little secretary, and they end up in a darling intimate little bar drinking Pink Ladies, and—"

I stopped listening. It would take a gag to shut her up, and so I strode around the desk and began to peer at the labels on the filing cabinets.

"—and they decided to get married, and be a detective team, and ... What in the world are you *doing?*"

"I'm looking for a goddamned list of students," I said, jerking open a file drawer. I slammed it shut, pulled out another.

"Well, you don't have to curse. My goodness. I—"

"Shut up," I snapped. "Please shut the hell up." I opened another drawer, slammed it shut, tried another.

"Hard," she breathed adoringly. "Hard and ruthless. How did you get that lovely scar on your cheek?"

I swung toward her. "Shaving. And I can damn soon get hard and ruthless if you don't get that goddamned list."

"A dream," she whispered swooningly, "a dream come true. Right out of the books, only better than the books. You're handsome in just the right roughneck sort of way, and your clothes are nice, but not too nice, just careless-like. Do you smoke a pipe? And do you have a big tobacco-smelling apartment full of books, and a bar, and albums of Chopin and Debussy?"

I said patiently, "Look, honey. I'm married and I got six kids. I can't meet my car payments and another kid is on the way. I belong to the Parent-Teacher Association, and I like hillbilly songs. I don't drink or smoke or stay out late at night. Now where the hell is that list?"

"You're joking," she said. "Really, I mean you are."

I moved slowly over to her and quietly and slowly I leaned down until our noses almost touched. She smelled nice and at this range her freckles looked as big as pennies. "Get me that list," I muttered.

She closed her eyes, tilted her face a little, and ran a pink tongue across her plump lower lip. "Kiss me," she whispered.

"Do I get that list?"

"Anything," she breathed. "Kiss me."

I kissed her. The kiss was nice, a little wet, but nice enough. But my heart wasn't in it, and I didn't drag it out. I backed away from her. "There, honey. Thank you very much. Now be a good girl and get that list."

She made fluttering motions at her hair. "Well," she said breathlessly. "My goodness."

"The list," I said gently.

She said poutingly, "I don't need any old list. I know who S.L. is."

I was speechless.

She picked up a yellow pencil, tapped the rubber end against her white front teeth, and smiled at me slyly. "I knew right away. It's Steve Lapham. He works in this office part time, to help with his tuition. He's a senior in the School of Science."

"Well, well," I said. "What do you know? And what branch of science, may I ask?"

"Archaeology. Prehistoric North America."

From out of the dark nowhere words came to me, two words, meaning nothing when I first heard them. Now they might mean something, or still nothing, but I had a faint stirring of excitement, the old feeling I loved. I remembered Vivian Prosper's report of her sister's babbling. It seemed like a long time ago. What was it? I thought hard, and I had it. "Pooh on your old

flint points." That was what Linda Prosper had babbled in her morphine and whisky delirium.

I said to the redhead, "'Flint point' is an expression
used by archaeological students, isn't it?"

"My goodness," she said. "Of course. Flint point is
another name for arrowhead. Indians, you know?
From being around Steve, I know that much. They
used to take flint and chip it into arrowheads and spear
points and cooking utensils—oh, all sorts of things.
Hundreds and hundreds of years ago. Steve told me all
about it. After he graduates, he wants to get attached
to some big museum, and make field trips to the dig-
gings, and give lectures, and write papers—all that sort
of thing."

"Very interesting," I said, "How well do you know
Steve Lapham?"

"Quite well. Really, I mean quite well. After all, we
work here together."

"Oh," I said. "Excuse me. Are you in love with
him?"

"Don't you wish you knew?" she said roguishly.
"Are you jealous?"

"Burning," I said. "When did you last see him?"

"You know what? I think I'm in love with you—all
of a sudden. Do you mind?"

"That's very sweet of you. I sincerely appreciate it.
Perhaps at a later date we can pursue our love in more
suitable surroundings. But—"

"In your apartment?" she asked eagerly. "With a
background of Chopin and Debussy?"

"Please, miss. I told you I was married. When did
you last see Steve Lapham?"

"You kissed me," she pouted. "You can't love your
wife very much if you did that. And my name is
Jacqueline. Stop calling me 'miss'. I think after kissing
me you can call me by my first name. I prefer Jackie.

Steve calls me Jackie. But I haven't seen him for a couple of days. He's probably cramming for some exams. Will you call me Jackie?"

"Sure, Jackie. What does Steve look like?" The excitement in me was mounting and I had a feeling that something was just beyond my reach, just across the border of darkness.

"Steve?" she said thoughtfully, and she put a finger to her lips. "Well, let's see. He has blue eyes and black hair, cut short, real cute, and he has a little scar across his nose. Why do you want to know about Steve?"

I had it then, and I knew I had it. A man dies with a knife in his chest, a girl is doped, another girl promises me paradise if I will help her hide a corpse. I don't help her, but still I get an unearned paradise. I talk to a brunette waitress named Blanche Dorinda Swickert in a place called the Venice Café and immediately afterward I get strangely and deathly sick and a boozy old doctor pulls me back into this world with a stomach pump. A scared old stepfather named Jerome K. Pitt tries to buy me away from Vivian Prosper, and I talk to a sensitive pale-faced pharmacist who should have been a poet, and who was weak enough and human enough to forsake his marriage vows and to embrace temptation in the form of a juvenile delinquent named Linda. I talk once more with Blanche Dorinda Swickert, and for cash, and certain other considerations, she promises to tell me things I burn to hear; but secret stalking death stills her over-red mouth forever, and I come at last to the hallowed halls of knowledge to learn that a dead man is named Steve Lapham.

It was one of the reasons why I wasn't selling life insurance, or sitting behind a desk, or making time studies of the man-minutes required to turn out an automobile fuel pump.

"Tell me," Jacqueline Hart said. "Why do you want to know about Steve? Is he in trouble?"

"No. Steve isn't in trouble. Where does he live?"

"He has a room in a private home somewhere near the campus, but I don't know where. I can give you the address, or—" She paused and looked at me thoughtfully.

"Or what?"

"You will probably find him at his girl friend's."

"Aren't you his girl friend?"

"Oh, no. We're just—uh—friendly, because we work together, and all."

"Give me his address anyhow."

"I will. But Dorothy will know where he is, if he isn't at his room, but what he sees in her I'll never understand. She keeps pretty close track of him—always calling up here to talk to him. She's been calling pretty often the last couple of days, to ask if he's been here. She must have found him, because she hasn't called since noon. But Steve is so handsome, and she—she's such a drip."

"What's wrong with Dorothy?"

"Oh, nothing," she said airily. "That is, if you like big girls, the buxom motherly type. She's majoring in home economics. All she thinks about is getting married and having two sets of twins. She probably will, too. But not to Steve. I've got a hunch that Steve will never marry her."

"I'm sure she won't marry Steve," I said grimly. "Where does Dorothy live?"

She smiled slyly. "What's it worth to you? Will you let me help you on a case? Can I be your secretary?"

"I can't afford a secretary."

"Oh, you don't have to *pay* me—not in money. Just let me go around with you, and hunt clues, and have drinks in cocktail lounges while we're tailing a suspect, and we'll take long rides in a convertible, and we'll talk and discuss clues and suspects, and you'll get a bottle of bourbon from the glove compartment, and—"

"I don't have a convertible," I told her. "I wouldn't have a damned convertible if I could afford one. I drive a Ford sedan. Now, how about those addresses?"

She got up and moved toward me. Her pink tongue was again flicking across her lower lip, and her eyes took on a veiled look. "Please," she said softly. "I mean it, really I do. I'd love to help you. Can I go with you tonight? I'll be through here at five-thirty."

By quick maneuvering I put the desk between us.

She started to follow me around it, but the opening door behind us stopped her. I turned. A slight little man with a black ribbon flowing from his glasses came in. He walked quickly past me and sat down at the big cluttered desk. "Good afternoon, Miss Hart," he said in a dry cracked voice, and he began to shuffle papers importantly.

"Good afternoon, Mr. Shawn," she said, moving back to her desk. As she sat down she gave me a warning glance.

I grinned at her and said, "If you'll just give me those addresses, I won't bother you any longer."

She bit her lip and hesitated.

Mr. Shawn looked at her over his glasses.

"Certainly, sir," she said. She stood up, moved to a file, thumbed through it, wrote briefly on a pad, tore off a sheet of paper, came back, and handed the sheet to me. I saw the names Stephen Lapham and Dorothy Toynbee and the street numbers.

"Thank you, miss," I said gravely, and I moved to the door. As I went out, I winked at her. She didn't wink back or smile, but just watched me with hot brooding eyes. She wasn't happy. I made a halfhearted mental note to look her up some lonely evening. After all, I was the only genuine private detective she'd ever met.

Chapter Eleven

A tired and vague old man sitting on the front porch of the house where Steve Lapham was supposed to have a room mumbled through a tobacco-stained white mustache that Stephen had not been in his room for a couple of days. I expected that, and I thanked him kindly and drove around the fringes of the campus to the house where Dorothy Toynbee lived. It had once been white, but now it was a flaky gray and one of the green shutters in front slanted away from a broken hinge. But the wide lawn had been recently cut, and fresh grass from the mower was strewn on the sidewalk that led up to a wide screened front porch. All of the windows, at least the ones facing the street, were bright and shining, and on the sills of two of the biggest windows geraniums bloomed gaily in freshly painted window boxes. A small sign on one of the porch pillars read: "Rooms for Students—Girls Only."

On the porch two girls were sitting on a wooden swing suspended by chains fastened in the ceiling. They were both small and dark, with identical straight-cut bangs across their foreheads, and they were dressed alike in white sweaters, dark green skirts, short white wool socks, brown moccasins. They were both licking at ice-cream cones, and they regarded me with bright-eyed interest.

"Hello, girls," I said.

"Hello," they said in unison.

"I'm looking for Dorothy Toynbee. Does she live here?"

"Yes," one of the girls said. The other one giggled.

I opened the screen door and stepped to the porch. "Is she here now?"

They looked at each other and they both giggled. The girl who had spoken took a lick at her cone and said, "Toyn is in her room. She's brooding."

"Is that what you call her? Toyn?"

They both nodded eagerly, licking at their cones. "I'd like to see her. What do I do—go right up to her room?"

"Heavens, no," the first girl said. "Mrs. Koppus won't stand for that. You'll have to ring for Mrs. Koppus. The bell's there by the door. After you prove that you aren't a white slaver, she'll probably have Toyn come down to the parlor."

"Thanks," I said.

The second girl spoke for the first time. "One good toyn deserves another," she said, and they giggled violently.

I pressed the button beside the door and waited. The two girls watched me expectantly, licking their cones. I said, "You girls twins?"

They both nodded vigorously, and one said, "I'm Mary."

The other said, "I'm Carrie."

"Mary and Carrie," I said admiringly. "What do you think of that? I once knew a set of boy twins named Pete and Repeat."

They giggled hilariously.

I was beginning to enjoy myself, and I said, "I know *another* set of twins named Taffy and Daffy."

That really brought the house down. They almost fell off the swing. In the midst of the gaiety, a cold voice said, "Yes?"

I turned back to the door. A stout woman stood gazing at me with a stern, inquiring expression. The sagging pouches beneath her eyes were the size of clam shells.

I took off my hat. "Mrs. Koppus?"

She nodded grimly, her heavy lips pursed. She was not an attractive woman. There was black hair on her upper lip and a single hair growing from a brown mole on her chin. Her black dress was spotted, and her stockings wrinkled above her thick ankles. With one hand she fingered a dime-store brooch at her throat, but I saw the glitter of two diamond rings on her fingers. Real diamonds. A stick of sunlight caught them and I almost had to shield my eyes.

I gave her my most charming smile. "My name is Brice," I said. "I wonder if I could see Miss Dorothy Toynbee for a few minutes."

She looked me over carefully and coldly, and apparently decided that I wasn't a white slaver. "Step into the parlor," she said. "I'll call her." Her voice, soft and pleasant, was the only attractive thing about her. Her voice, and the diamonds.

"Thank you, madam."

Her lips quivered in what might have been a smile. She turned, and I followed her down a wide hall filled with vases and urns and wicker baskets from which sprouted a variety of ivies and flowing weedlike vines. A few of the containers held cut flowers, most of them wilted, and they filled the hall with a dank smell.

Mrs. Koppus said over her shoulder, "Do you like my display? Whenever I send flowers to a funeral I always ask the undertaker to save the vases or the baskets for me. I'm getting quite a collection."

"Very attractive," I murmured.

We passed an old-fashioned umbrella stand, a hall tree with brass prongs imitating a deer's antlers, a tall grandfather clock with the brass weights hanging mathematically even and with the hands stopped probably years ago at the hour of two o'clock. At the far end of the hall Mrs. Koppus stopped and pushed back a sliding door and ushered me into a cool, musty-smelling room crowded almost to suffocation with chairs, divans, hassocks, small tables, and settees. Countless framed photographs decorated the walls, the top of an upright piano, and the tables. Old people, young people, large groups, small groups, all posed with set expressions as they fixedly watched the picture-snapper.

There were numerous small china pots, mostly in the shapes of dogs, elephants, and birds, sprouting cacti, shrubs, and vines. There were no funeral baskets here. They were apparently restricted to the hall, where visitors could be impressed with Mrs. Koppus' generosity to the dead. On a small mantel over a gas-burning fireplace was a bulbous glass jar filled with water in which was submerged a pallid sweet potato from which curled green octopus-like tendrils in a frightening confusion out over the top of the jar and onto the floor.

Mrs. Koppus said in her pleasant voice, "Are you from the college?"

"No, ma'am."

"Then you don't know Stephen Lapham?"

I tried to conceal my surprise at the question, and said carefully, "No, ma'am," which was the truth.

She sighed heavily. "That poor girl. She's going to cry herself sick abed if he don't show up. She's been carrying on for two days now—just stays in her room, and she won't eat a thing, and I fixed her chicken and biscuit, this noon." She sighed again. "I was hoping that maybe you had news for her about Stephen. Are you a friend of Dorothy's?"

"Not exactly. I just want to see her for a minute— a business matter."

She backed through the doorway. "Well, I'll see if I can get her to come down." She hesitated, her lips broadening into a smile, and said, "Young man, who taught you to take off your hat in the presence of a lady? Your mother?"

"I guess so," I said, thinking of my mother, who had been dead for ten years.

"I like that," she said. "Nobody has any manners any more. She brought you up right." She turned and went out, and I heard her slow muffled steps on a carpeted stairway.

I sat carefully on a thin-legged chair with a worn brocaded seat. I didn't see any ash trays, so I didn't light a cigarette. I twirled my hat in my hands and wondered what the twins on the front porch were doing. I wished they were here in this dead museum of a room to talk to me. I waited maybe ten minutes, and I began to get restless. I didn't like what I had to do and I wanted to get it over with. Then I heard slow steps coming down the stairs. I stood up as a girl moved slowly into the room.

Jacqueline Hart in the college registrar's office had been right. Dorothy Toynbee was buxom, all right—just a shade too buxom for her marital status. She had been a big girl to begin with, and pregnancy had not slimmed her any. She was not far along; my unpracticed eye estimated the time at about three to four months. But far enough along to show, at least to those looking for it.

She was wearing a soft red-and-blue print dress, scuffed saddle oxfords, no stockings. A fine fuzz of blonde hair glinted on her sturdy legs below the hem of her dress.

But Dorothy Toynbee would never be glamorous; she wasn't the type. I gave Jacqueline Hart grudging credit for her perspicacity. Dorothy Toynbee was pretty, in a rather full-blown way, but she was definitely the home-and-baby type of girl; large-boned, soft, maybe slightly bovine, with big soft breasts and wide hips. She had tawny yellow hair streaked with a darker tan, a full face with a round chin, a short nose, a full soft red mouth. Her velvet brown eyes were red-rimmed from two days of sobbing. Her lips looked swollen, and the end of her nose was faintly red. She stared at me sullenly.

"Miss Toynbee?" I asked.

She fingered a thin gold chain around her neck. The end of the chain disappeared beneath the print dress into the V between her breasts. "What do you want?" she said in a dead voice.

I hesitated. How to begin? I cleared my throat. "Uh—you are a friend of Stephen Lapham?"

A faint gleam entered her dull eyes. "Yes," she said, trying to control her voice. "Why?" The big breasts moved with quickened breathing, and she watched me hopefully and expectantly.

I felt sorry for her, as sorry as all hell. I motioned her to a chair. "Won't you sit down?"

She moved slowly past me, and I was aware of the pleasant smell of her, like sunshine and freshly mowed hay and warm sweet milk. She sat down, stiff, erect, with her toes turned slightly inward. Already she was instinctively sitting a little straddle-legged. Her big soft brown eyes watched me silently. There was the beginning of fear in them now, even a hint of terror. Her soft pink mouth moved once, but she didn't speak.

I said gently, "When did you last see him?"

"S-Steve?"

I nodded.

"Two nights ago. He—" She stopped abruptly, and I could almost feel her pulling her nerves into line.

"Steve's in trouble, isn't he?" Her voice rose. "Isn't he? That's why he didn't come back to me as he promised."

"I don't know," I said. "I—"

"*What's happened to him?*" She whispered the words, but they held the impact of a shout.

I was as sure as I would ever be, but I couldn't tell her, not yet. The years seem to have done something to me, softened me too much, maybe, and I couldn't tell her at that moment that her Steve was dead. I would have to tell her in the end, but the end wasn't just yet, and I said, "I want to help you. Do you have a photo of Steve?"

She plucked at the thin gold chain and lifted a gold locket from between her breasts. She held it lovingly and caressingly for a moment, and then she opened it and turned it toward me. "That's Steve," she said quietly and proudly.

I had to move close to her and bend over to get a good look, and again I was aware of her clean sweet scent. The photo was a clear snapshot, taken in the sun, with the head cut into a small disc to fit in the locket. It was the man, all right, the same man I'd found in Linda's car. I could even make out the scar on his nose. I knew it would be, but still it came as kind of a surprise. It was like hitting the jackpot, or being dealt four aces. Now the wheels would turn, the real work would start, the main event was about to come out under the lights. The hunt was on, with the old excitement mounting in me, and I knew once more that I wouldn't switch jobs with any deskbound clock-watcher for anything in the world.

Dorothy Toynbee looked up at me. I was close enough to her to see the tiny tan flecks in her brown eyes. "Steve's in trouble, isn't he?"

I still felt sorry for her, but now I was thinking ahead, my mind racing beyond this musty room to the people I must see, the places I must go. Dorothy Toynbee was just a signpost along the road I must travel, someone who could give me information that I would need, someone to use and to forget about and then maybe remember and return to, if I had to. I burned to be on my way, but first I must bleed her, squeeze all I could out of her, before I told her that Steve wasn't in trouble, not any more, that Steve's troubles were over for good.

I said, "Tell me about what happened when you last saw Steve."

"Where is he? What's happened?"

"I don't know," I lied. "I'm trying to find out."

"Are you a policeman?"

"Yes," I lied again.

She beat her fists on her knees. "Why do you want to know about Steve?"

My mind began to formulate the smooth words of another lie. And then I thought to hell with it. She's in love with him, and he got her pregnant, and he's never coming back to her. She had a right to know, and I might as well tell her. I intended to speak gently and kindly to her, to show her that I was sorry, but my voice sounded harsh in my ears. "You may as well know. Steve is dead."

I had to shoot a horse one time, when I was a kid on my father's farm. She was an old mare and no good any more for breeding or for work. Her name was Stella and for many years my father kept her in the greenest pasture in the summer, and in the warmest part of the barn in the winter, until one spring she fell in a ditch against some barbed wire and cut a big vein in her neck and broke her left foreleg. Crops had been bad that year and my father hated to spend the money for a vet, but still he wouldn't shoot the mare, and I had to. I remembered the look in Stella's eyes as I raised the rifle. It was the same look that I now saw in the soft brown eyes of Dorothy Toynbee.

Her lips moved silently, and then she whisper "D-dead …?"

"Yes. Yesterday morning he was found stabbed to death in the rear compartment of a car belonging to a girl named Linda Prosper. Does that mean anything to you?"

"I loved him. We were going to get married."

"Linda Prosper," I said softly. "Where does she fit in?"

She moved in the chair, turning away from me. Her dress twisted up above her knees and I saw the smooth swelling expanse of milk-white thighs and the faint blue of veins. She covered her face with her hands, strong hands with clear unpainted nails, and her soft

ripe body shook with uncontrolled sobs. I lit a cigarette, ash trays or no ash trays, and for a time there
was no other sound in the musty crowded room but
Dorothy Toynbee's choking, strangled weeping.

I let her cry. The cigarette was burning my fingers
before she stopped. I put it out on the sole of my shoe
and dropped it into one of the cactus vases. Dorothy
Toynbee gazed at me hopelessly, her eyes red, her face
swollen and wet with tears. I got up and moved over
to her, placed a hand on one round soft shoulder. Her
chin began to quiver, like a baby's, but she didn't cry
any more. She was saving it now for when she was
alone in her room.

"Good girl," I said, patting her shoulder. "I'm very
sorry. Tell me about it, all of it, and you'll feel better."

She sighed brokenly and sat heavily in the chair,
knees slightly spread, feet toed in, hands clasped in her
lap. She lowered her head and her thick tawny hair fell
forward over her face. She began to talk in a low dead
voice.

"I loved Steve, and he loved me. I think he did, he
said he did. We were going to get married as soon as
he graduated at the end of the summer term, and
then—then we decided to get married sooner—right
away. Then he told me that he was already married, to
a girl named Linda Prosper. They eloped to Kentucky
after a drinking party, to a town called Greenup. That
was six months ago, before he met me. Afterward
Steve said he knew that it was a mistake, and after he
met me he asked her for a divorce, so that he could
marry me. She refused, and—"

"Why?" I asked.

She looked at me dully through the hanging hair.
"I don't know," she said. "Something about her age
and her sister not liking it, and the publicity, Steve said.
Must I go on with this?"

"You must, if you want Steve's killer nabbed," I
said.

"I do, I do! Do you think *she* did it?" She was incapable of real anger, a soft girl like her, but for an instant her soft eyes didn't look soft, and a tiny devil prodded my brain. She was hefty enough to push a knife into Steve Lapham, and she had plenty of motive—more than plenty.

"I don't know," I answered her. "Were you with Steve the night before last?"

"A little while—a very little while. He came here early in the evening. He was excited. He said he had arranged to meet Linda and have it out with her, to ask her once more for a quiet divorce. If she refused, he was going ahead and sue for divorce, whether she wanted him to or not. You see, we had to hurry—" She stopped and blushed. It had slipped out.

"Then what?" I asked gently.

"Steve promised to come back to me after he'd talked to Linda. I waited until morning. I—I didn't know what to think. Yesterday afternoon I walked over to where Steve lives, but he hadn't been there. I cut classes and stayed in my room. I didn't know what to do. Last night I called every Prosper in the phone book until a woman at one of them told me that Linda was ill and couldn't talk to anyone. Then I gave up and just waited." She brushed the hair back with a listless hand. "Where is Steve now?"

I almost said, "Lying on a slab in the city morgue," but I checked myself and said instead, "He's all right. We'll take care of him."

"Could—could I see him?"

"We may need you for identification."

"I want to see him," she said plaintively.

"We'll see," I said soothingly. "Just wait here."

I left her sitting there in her pregnancy and her grief and I stepped out into the hall lined with funeral baskets. At the far end Mrs. Koppus was puttering around one of the baskets. She turned immediately. I didn't know how close she had been hanging around the door, or how much she had heard. It didn't make any difference. I said to her, "Dorothy is in trouble."

"I know it," she said calmly. "You're from the police, aren't you?"

"Yes." It was the easiest answer. "Her boy friend, Stephen Lapham, has been murdered."

"Murdered?" The single black hair in the center of the brown mole quivered.

"Yes, ma'am."

"Oh, the poor girl! The poor, poor girl!"

I said delicately, "You were aware of her—uh—condition?"

"Of course. Girls can never fool me. As a matter of fact, I was beginning to wonder what to do about it. I feel a sense of responsibility for my girls, you know."

"It's a rough deal for her," I said. "She seems like a nice girl. Where is her home?"

"In Wisconsin. Her parents are quite wealthy. They operate a huge dairy farm near Madison. Do you want me to get in touch with them?"

"Yes, but you'd better wait until the police get here. Did she go out the night before last?"

"I don't think so. There was a light in her room until after midnight, and I heard her walking about. She could have gone out after I went to bed. ... I thought you said you were a policeman."

"I'm just a detective. I'm going to call my sergeant now. Where's the phone?"

She pointed into a little alcove at the front end of the hall.

I jerked my head toward the room where I'd left Dorothy Toynbee. "Maybe you'd better take her up to her room and stay with her."

She nodded. "You know, I thought you were a policeman when I first saw you. And then you removed your hat, and I wasn't so sure."

I smiled at her. "Some cops are polite." I moved into the alcove. From the end of the hall I heard the murmur of Mrs. Koppus' voice as she spoke to Dorothy Toynbee. I wasn't worried about the girl's skipping. She wasn't the skipping kind, and besides, Mrs. Koppus would keep an eye on her.

Chapter Twelve

I caught Detective Sergeant Dave Navarre in his office.
I told him that I'd learned the identity of the corpse in
Linda's car, that I'd located the corpse's wronged girl
friend, and I told him where I was.

He didn't waste time in asking questions. He just
said, "Thanks, Andy, I'll be right out."

As I walked out of the alcove I saw Mrs. Koppus
going up the stairs with her arm around Dorothy
Toynbee. I went to the porch to wait and I was disap-
pointed to find that the twins were gone.

In fifteen minutes Navarre pulled up in a squad car
driven by a uniformed cop. I went out to the curb to
meet him and we went back to the porch together and
sat on the steps. "The landlady's with the girl," I told
him, "so relax."

He was smoking a cigar. I lit a cigarette and gave
him a complete story of my day's activities, every de-
tail, from the time Jerome K. Pitt visited me to my talk
with Dorothy Toynbee. The only thing I omitted was
the fact that I'd slept with Vivian Prosper, and I figured
that was not police business. I told him of my visit to
the apartment of Allan Frederick Keeler, of my brief
but eventful acquaintance with Blanche Dorinda
Swickert, and of my talk with Jacqueline Hart, which
had led me to Dorothy Toynbee. I gave it to him
straight, all of it. I never did see any point in holding
out on the cops. Sometimes I was tempted, but in the
long run it wasn't worth it. I liked the cops. The only
reason I wasn't in the detective division myself was because it didn't pay enough.

When I had finished, Navarre turned his dark lean
face toward me and grinned with the cigar between his
teeth. "You've had a busy day, huh, Andy?"

"You said it, Sarge."

"Me, too," he sighed. "I guess I've just been a jump behind you all day, except that I talked to Arthur Spotwood, the gas-station guy who's nuts about that Linda gal. And I saw the stepfather, Jerome Pitt, and I talked some more with the older sister—what's her name?"

"Vivian."

"She steered me onto her ex-husband, this Keeler, and I talked to him. So you called in that Swickert kill?"

"Yeah."

"Any ideas?"

I shook my head. "Not any that are good. Somebody didn't want her to talk to me—that's as good as I can do. Or maybe it would have happened anyhow."

"Two killings," Navarre said softly. "Both with knives. I hope we can stop the third one."

"Why three?"

He shrugged. "I don't know. It always seems to run that way. Where there's two, it often ends up three. Don't ask me why."

I shivered a little. Who was going to be number three? Navarre flung his cigar out over the grass. "Does this Toynbee gal have an alibi?"

"Not airtight. And she had a good reason for killing Lapham. He got her pregnant and then told her he couldn't marry her because he was already married to Linda Prosper. But I don't think she killed him."

"Why the hell not?"

"She's not the killing kind. She's the gentle milkmaid type. Her folks own a dairy farm in Wisconsin."

"That's no reason. I'll work on her."

"Remember her condition."

"Oh, I will," he said impatiently. "What about that phone number and Lapham's initials you took from Keeler's apartment? Did he write 'em down?"

I took the paper from my pocket and handed it to him. "Check the handwriting, if it'll help any. But it could have been written by whoever was snooping around his place before he came home. They had to slug him from behind to get away."

"Toynbee's my gal," Navarre said, "pregnant or not. Jealousy is the motive."

"A girl can't afford to be jealous when she's pregnant," I said.

He laughed softly. "We'll see, Andy." He stood up.

I looked at my wrist watch. Ten minutes until six in the afternoon. "Look, Dave, I've got a date. I'll see you."

"Aren't you going to stick around?"

I shook my head, and then I thought of something. "Hey, did you check on Keeler's story about being at the drive-in movie the night before last?"

"Of course," he said. "My God, that's routine. I found out that the feature was Toni Lord in 'The Devil's Price', if that's what you mean. But it's no alibi. The movie didn't last *all* night."

"No, but it proves that Keeler is sincere."

"I'm not overlooking anything, Andy."

"What about Kentucky marriage laws?" I asked him. "I haven't eloped lately, and I'm a little fuzzy. Could Lapham and Linda get married that fast?"

"Sure. Kentucky law permits a girl as young as sixteen to get married without establishing residence and without parent's or guardian's consent. I'll check it pretty quick. Greenup is the town, you said?"

"Yeah."

He opened the screen door and stepped up to the porch. "Thanks for calling me, Andy."

"You're welcome," I said, and I walked out to my car. It was all sweetness and light between Sergeant Navarre and me, and that was the way I wanted it.

I drove the six miles across town to my apartment, put my car in the garage in the rear, and went up the back stairs without bothering with the elevator. There was a note from the switchboard under my door. "Mr.

Brice: Please call Dr. L. M. Otten, Lakeside 2098." The time marked on the note was 4:20 P.M.

I called the number, got no answer. I hung up, made a mental note to call later, and entered my bedroom. It was almost six-thirty. Vivian had said she'd be here around six. I took off my coat, shirt, and tie and went to the bathroom. The mirror told me that my shave earlier in the day would last a while yet. So I washed my face, combed my hair, brushed my teeth, and put on a clean shirt. I was in the process of tying a red-speckled bow tie, and I had just succeeded in making the ends come out even, when the apartment buzzer sounded. Vivian was late, but she was here, and that was good enough for me.

But it wasn't Vivian. Arthur Spotwood stood there with a mean look in his eye. He was breathing heavily and his fists were clenched. I backed away a little. If he swung one of the fists, I wanted a little room to maneuver.

"Come in," I invited, but I was just trying to save face, because he was already in and backed up against the slammed door and looking at me as if I were something crawling to be stepped on. He was wearing a pair of grease-stained G.I. suntan trousers and a tan shirt with "Spotwood's Super Service" stitched in red across the pocket. He needed a shave, and his blond hair needed a combing.

"Well," I said, "get it off your chest."

"You told them, damn you."

"Told who what?"

"The police. You told them that I was with Linda that night. They had me downtown. Questions, questions."

"What're you worried about?" I asked curiously. "Don't you have an alibi for what you did after Linda left you?"

"Alibi?" He looked bewildered. "I'm not thinking of myself. It's Linda I'm worried about."

"Can you prove what you did after she left you?"

"Goddamn it," he shouted, "I don't have to prove
it! You're all against me, you and Vivian and the police."

"Jerome's on your side," I said softly.

That got him. But only for a second. Then he said,
"That drunken Jerome has been talking to you."

"I know about your deal with him."

"What's wrong with it?" he asked defiantly. "Jerome wants the money, and I want Linda. If he can
help to make up her mind to marry me, he's welcome
to Linda's money. I don't want it. I just want Linda,
and by God, I'm going to get her, and you and Vivian
and nobody else is going to stop me."

"Even if you're forced to kill off her other boy
friends to get her?" I asked.

I had intended to needle him, but I didn't expect
him to react so violently. He uttered a low, almost animal cry of rage and lunged for me, his fists high and
already jabbing before he reached me. I didn't move
fast enough and one of his fists ripped across my
mouth and I tasted blood. I stumbled backward, trying
to cover up, but it was like trying to ward off a hurri-
cane. Knuckles ripped across my left ear and a fist battered my chest. I caught a quick glimpse of his face,
contorted with the wild blind fury of a ten-year-old de-
fending his new football from the neighborhood bully.
Then he had me against the wall, his fists hammering
away at me. I couldn't even get my arms clear to start
a punch at him.

There was only one thing to do. I brought up my
knee, hard and fast, into his stomach. It worked. He
doubled over, gasping and wheezing for breath, and
stumbled and lurched in a wide circle around my living
room. I went into the bedroom, got a flat .32 Smith
and Wesson automatic from the dresser drawer, and
returned. Spotwood was still doubled over, still gasping. I let him gasp and entered the bathroom. The cut

on my lip wasn't much, but my ear hurt to beat hell. It
was red and beginning to swell. Cold water felt good
on it. In a couple of minutes I returned to the living
room, with the .32 in my hip pocket.

Spotwood was sprawled in a chair. He was breathing hard and his face beneath the tan was the color of
good bond paper. I stood in the middle of the room
and pointed a finger at him. "You going to behave?" I
asked him.

"Where—where did you learn that trick?" he
panted.

I grinned. "Like it? I learned it in the Army. My
first sergeant taught me. One night in a bar in Bor-
deaux it came in real handy. Other times, too."

He looked surprised. "You're a G.I.?"

"Five years, six months, and fourteen days."

"Me, too," he said. "Army Air Corps."

"Just a couple of buddies. What was your rating?"

"You mean rank," he said, smiling. "First Lieutenant. Fighter pilot."

I gave him a sharp salute. "Corporal Brice, sir. In-
fantry."

He leaned forward, tenderly felt his stomach, and
took a deep breath. "Sorry I blew my top," he said.
"I—I'm all mixed up." He looked up at me. A little
color had come back into his face. "Now, listen. Somebody planted that dead man in Linda's car. She
wouldn't kill a man, no matter what you or the police
think. I talked to her, but I couldn't get anything sen-
sible out of her, except that you and Vivian are working together. The police didn't tell me anything, either—not even who the dead man is. Who is he? What
is he?"

I said, "The police didn't tell you because they
didn't know. They know now. His name was Steve
Lapham." I paused, and decided to let him have it. "He
was Linda's husband."

He gazed dumbly at me for a long moment. I felt sorry for him, and I wanted to look away. What was in his eyes was something personal and private. It was a little like what I'd seen in the eyes of Dorothy Toynbee, and in the eyes of the old mare I'd shot years ago.

At last he said in a tight strained voice, "You're lying. Linda isn't old enough to get married. Not without Vivian's consent."

"She was married in Kentucky, under Kentucky law. The police are checking it."

He took a deep shuddering breath. "Did Vivian know that? Is that why she tried to keep me away from Linda?"

"I don't know. If she knew it, she didn't tell me."

"That—that's a shock, I'll admit," he said, and he took a deep breath. "But it doesn't matter now. He's dead, and I've got to help Linda. You're in cahoots with Vivian, but did she tell you that unless Linda marries within a year after her eighteenth birthday, and stays married, her share of the estate goes to her, Vivian, and that she continues as legal guardian, to hand out the money as she sees fit? A nice setup for Vivian, if she can keep Linda from marrying. Did she tell you that?"

I had to admit that she hadn't.

He laughed shortly. "Vivian's sharp, all right. Always looking out for Vivian. If it hadn't been for her, Linda and I would have been married long ago and none of this would have happened. But Vivian wouldn't give her consent, because she wanted Linda's share of the estate, and because she's crazy jealous of her and she doesn't want her to have any happiness. She made a mess of her own marriage, and she's determined that Linda won't have a chance to make a success of hers. Vivian is a selfish, greedy, jealous bitch. I know her very well, and—"

"Hold it," I broke in, and I thought mockingly of the old gag line, "You're talking about the woman I love." I had a good notion to tell him that Linda had caused Vivian's marriage to go on the rocks, but I didn't. I said, "You had a pretty good reason yourself for eliminating Linda's husband."

He clenched his fists and said evenly, "I still think you're a heel—G.I. or not."

"Very good, Lieutenant. Does this conclude our interview?" I didn't want Vivian to find him here, if she was coming. I looked at my watch. A quarter of seven.

"Expecting someone?" Spotwood said mockingly.

"How about you getting the hell out?"

He stood up. "Glad to. I need some fresh air."

"Get it," I said, and I opened the door.

In the hall he turned and said in a tight voice, "How about a return engagement? Will you teach me that stomach-punch trick?"

"Any time, Lieutenant." I closed the door.

In the kitchen I got out my fancy cut-glass cocktail set and stirred up a pitcher of Martinis. When they were good and cold I sampled one while I opened a can of cleaned shrimp, mixed the sauce, and arranged a glass plate with crackers and olives. I even remembered the toothpicks in the olives and shrimp. Then I poured myself another Martini, placed the pitcher in the refrigerator, and carried my drink to the telephone. Once more I tried to get Dr. Otten at Lakeside 2098. Still no answer. Right after I hung up, the phone jangled.

It was Vivian Prosper. "You're supposed to be here," I told her. "You're late."

"I'm sorry," she said, and I thought her voice was a trifle cool, "but I think it would be better to meet you somewhere."

"Better, hell. I've got a pitcher of Martinis in the icebox and a luscious plate of canapés all ready."

"We can have a drink here," she said.

"Here? Where the hell are you?"

"The Venice Café."

"Why, for God's sake?"

"After what you told me, I decided to do a little investigating of my own."

"That's silly. You're paying me to do the investigating. Besides, you'll get in trouble in that dump. Don't drink any of their Manhattans."

"I'm drinking one right now. Are you coming, or aren't you? Do you have anything to report?"

"Plenty. Let's skip the date, and I'll report right now."

"Don't be childish. Not on the phone."

"Then you'd better come here," I said firmly.

"I prefer not to."

For an instant I had a strong desire to hang up. To hell with her. Why was she getting so coy all of a sudden? But like millions of other trapped males, I remembered the pleasure of the night before and I swallowed my pride and my anger and said, "All right. I'll be there. Sit tight." I hung up, sneering at myself.

Chapter Thirteen

The yellow sun of early evening filled the street as I stepped out of the apartment building. The traffic had thinned out and half of the street was in the shade of the buildings on the far side. The city was in that brief calm called the dinner hour, the time spent between the after-work cocktails and the first highball of the evening. Soon the lights would come on and the bars would come to life; the movie marquees would proclaim their offerings in glittering lights, the bigger-than-life photos of the strippers in front of the burlesque houses would glow warmly as the bare bulbs illuminated the rosy painted flesh. Soon the drunks would stumble out of the alleys, and sharp-faced men in flashy suits would eye the passing women hoping for a pickup for maybe the price of a couple of drinks. Horns would bleat while the traffic curdled in the street and the dark would come in off the lake and another night in the city would begin.

But now it was quiet, peaceful, almost pastoral, a time of the day I liked. I stepped to the sidewalk and turned toward the corner, thinking that rather than get my car out of the garage I'd take a taxi to the Venice Café. Behind me in the quiet street a car motor roared from idling speed into first gear and above the snarl of the motor there was a sharp crack and brick dust puffed from the wall beside me. Without thinking or looking, I dropped flat to the sidewalk as three some-things went *splat, splat, splat* against the wall above me. I hugged the cement, waiting for the next bullet. I thought of my gun in my apartment, but thinking of it wouldn't help me, and I sweated it out, remembering wildly the beach at Anzio.

But no more shots came. I heard the angry whine of the motor, and I risked raising my head, but I was too low; the cars parked at the curb obscured my view of the street. All I saw was a blur of movement and from the corner there came a screech of tires. Some-body yelled and I heard running footsteps. Slowly I pushed myself to my feet and began to brush dust from the new gray suit I'd worn for Vivian Prosper.

A voice said, "Hey, you all right?"

I looked into the wide-eyed face of a husky kid in a white T shirt. Across the front of the shirt were the words "South Side High—Fight Team!"

"I'm all right, sonny,"

I said. "Did you see that car?"

He shook his head. "Didn't see no car. I heard what sounded like backfires, but faster than backfires, and I saw you hit the sidewalk and I came running."

"No car—going fast?" I pointed at the corner. "It turned there."

He shook his head. "I was looking the other way." He looked at the brick wall, saw the four chipped de-pressions. "Jeez! Bullets?"

"Yeah." I took a deep breath. I was feeling a little steadier, but bullets are unnerving things. A small curious crowd was beginning to gather. I ducked back into the apartment building and took the elevator up. I gulped some Martini from the pitcher in the refrigerator, washed my hands, and finished brushing off my suit. Then I dropped my .32 into my inside coat pocket. A gun can get you into trouble, maybe, but nevertheless it was a nice comfortable weight against my ribs. I went back down to the street.

A cruise car was angled into the curb and a couple of cops had pushed back the crowd and were examining the brick wall. The kid in the T shirt was talking excitedly. I knew one of the cops. "Hello, Andy," he said, grinning. "Somebody gunning for you?"

"Yeah." I was still a little shaky.

He held out a palm and showed me a small flattened chunk of lead. "I found one of the slugs," he said. "Looks like a .22. That isn't much gun. He must have thought he was good. What happened?"

I told him, said I had no idea who it had been, that I couldn't describe the car. He took it all down in a notebook, stuck the book into a hip pocket, hitched at his gun belt, and said, "Well, that's it, I guess. He's probably halfway to Buffalo by now." He grinned at me. "Why would anybody be gunning for you, Andy? A nice, friendly shamus like you? You got enemies, huh?"

"Could be," I said. "You never know."

"Probably some poor bastard of a husband," he said, still grinning. "Some guy whose wife wanted to marry the chauffeur or the butler or somebody, and you rigged a divorce for her. How about it, hey?"

"Please," I said stiffly. "You've been reading too many books. You know I never do divorce work."

He laughed and patted my arm. "Take it easy, Andy." He got into the cruiser with the other cop and drove away. A hell of a note, I thought bitterly. I get shot at on the public streets and all the cops do is laugh and make unfunny jokes. Still feeling hurt, scared, and worried, I pushed my way through the gawkers and flagged a taxi at the corner.

She was sitting at the bar in the Venice Café. She looked as if she'd been there for a long time. As I entered, she slid off the stool and came toward me with a long-legged graceful stride, her long yellow hair flowing in smooth folds over her shoulders. Her lime-green dress was low in the neckline, tight over her breasts and waist, and full over her hips. With her golden skin, red mouth, and off-green eyes she was a pleasure to behold. Over one arm hung a straw basket-like purse with a clasp top, and in her hand was a half-consumed Manhattan cocktail.

I decided to keep it friendly, if I could, and I smiled at her. "Hi."

She didn't smile back. "You're late," she said. She moved to a booth along the wall and sat down. I sat down opposite her. The place brought back memories of the two previous afternoons, today's and yesterday's, and the sight of Vivian Prosper's Manhattan and the smell of frying fish created a combination that, for a second, almost nauseated me. My throat was still a little tender.

A waitress came over, and I thought sadly of Blanche Dorinda Swickert. This girl was slender with a long nose and a frizzy hair-do. "Where's Blanche?" I asked her.

"She's on the first shift—seven to three. She'll be here in the morning."

"No, she won't," I said.

She lifted her thin shoulders. "They come and go. You wanna order?"

Vivian Prosper was watching me curiously. I looked away from her and said to the waitress, "A Manhattan and a double Martini." She left a couple of menus and moved over to the bar. Beneath the white uniform her hips were like two grapefruits on a board.

I reached across the table and picked up the basket purse. Vivian made a sudden movement to prevent me, but I had it in my lap and was unclasping the top. There was a gun inside, the flat little silver-plated automatic I'd taken away from her and then returned. Holding it beneath the table, I released the cartridge clip and saw that it was full of bright brass bullets. I checked the firing chamber, saw a cartridge in position. The safety was on. I leaned down and smelled the muzzle. I knew I was supposed to do things like that, but it didn't mean anything to me. The gun could have been fired five minutes ago, or last week, for all I knew. I replaced it in the purse, pushed the purse across the table, and smiled at Vivian Prosper.

"All finished snooping?" she asked coldly.

"What's the matter with you?" I asked her. "When we got out of bed this morning everything was fine." It wasn't a very nice thing to say, but her manner irritated me.

She flushed and avoided my gaze. "I—I'm sorry, Andy. I'm worried and upset. Things are bad. You know that. Sergeant Navarre came to see me a while ago. That's why I was late in calling you." She raised her gaze to mine, and she really looked worried. "He told me that the—the man in Linda's car was her husband. They were married in Greenup, Kentucky, six months ago. Navarre telephoned there and verified it. His name is Stephen Lapham. I asked Linda about it, in Sergeant Navarre's presence, and she broke down and admitted it. But she won't tell us anything else— says she can't remember. She's still in her room. There's a policeman in the house, and two outside." She reached out and touched my hand. "Andy, you've got to do something."

"Did Navarre tell you anything else?"

"Yes. He said that you had uncovered the evidence identifying the man, and had learned of the marriage."

Good old Dave, I thought, my favorite cop. Credit where credit is due, none of this hogging the laurels. "What else?" I asked her.

"That's all he told me. Is there something more I should know?"

I shook my head. Apparently Navarre hadn't told her about Blanche Dorinda Swickert or Dorothy Toynbee, and I decided to string along with him and keep quiet, too. I said, "You may as well face it. Linda is on a very hot spot."

She said scornfully, "I suppose a little girl like Linda stabs a big man to death, and then puts him in her car and brings him home with her?"

I shrugged. "She was drunk and doped, and she could have done almost anything and not remember it. And as for getting him into her car, sometimes small persons are stronger than you think, especially under stress. Besides, someone could have helped her. She was with *two* men, remember. Lapham and someone else, at least while they were here."

"Oh, stop it," she snapped. "Why are you so determined to implicate my sister in murder?"

"I'm trying to learn the truth," I said. "That's what you wanted, wasn't it?"

"Yes, of course. I suppose you're going to ask next which one of her many boy friends she wanted to marry, and which one would want to marry her badly enough to help her get rid of her husband?"

"*Many* boy friends?"

The skinny-hipped waitress brought our drinks then, and Vivian waited until she had moved languidly away before she answered. Then she said bitterly, "Little Linda likes variety. The ones I happen to know about include Arthur Spotwood, of course, and a tennis player from Cleveland, a dark man from God knows where who drives a Rolls-Royce roadster, an airline pilot from Texas whose schedule puts him in town twice a week, a couple of unidentified boys with crew haircuts and jalopies, and Allan, of course, and—I even caught Jerome kissing her in the garage one afternoon."

"Your stepfather?"

"Nice family, don't you think?"

"Who's Allan?" I asked, before I remembered.

"Allan Keeler," she said in a brittle voice, "my dear ex-husband. He's been hanging around Linda since I divorced him. Linda's boasted and taunted me about it several times."

I pulled a hand down over my face. Weren't there any nice, normal, Sunday-chicken-dinner people in the world anymore? Or was it just because my work brought me into contact with the wrong kind? I took a drink of the double Martini, and when I put the glass down it wasn't a double anymore; it wasn't even a respectable single Martini. It didn't help. Nothing ever helps when you try to cope with the things that people can do when they're driven by love, or the absence of love, or greed, or revenge, or hate, or any of the things that lead in one way or another to the final crime of murder.

I said wearily, "With so many boy friends and potential husbands, why are you so worried about Arthur Spotwood in particular?"

She hadn't touched her fresh drink and she was watching me with a bright intensity. "Because she's with him more than the rest," she said. "Because, for some reason, Jerome has been building him up to Linda, trying to throw them together. And Linda has told me that she intends to marry him—eventually. She said he was just stupid enough to make her a good faithful husband—after she's through with what she calls fun. But I don't think Arthur's so stupid. I think he's got his eyes on that damned money she'll get from Mother's estate."

Remembering what Arthur Spotwood had told me, I thought of a remark to make to her, but I didn't make it. I said, "Maybe not. Maybe it's true love."

"Love," she sneered. "What do you know about love?"

She was certainly in a nasty mood. "Not much," I admitted, "except when it's mixed up with murder. A lot of killing is done in the name of love." I finished my drink, and as I fished for the two olives I added, "I don't think you know much about love, either."

For an instant there was a softening in her eyes. "Maybe not," she said quietly. "Maybe love is something I have to look forward to."

"We live on hope," I said. "Want another drink?"

"Yes. Do you?"

I nodded at her full glass. "Then you'd better finish that one."

She lifted her glass, and for the first time she smiled.

It was a little better after that, but not much. We had another drink, and we ate something, I don't remember what, and we didn't talk much. The gun in her purse wasn't mentioned, and I didn't tell her of the four bullets whispering death at me on their way to the brick wall, or of Arthur Spotwood's visit. I didn't tell her of my conversation with Jerome K. Pitt, or of my visit to Allan Frederick Keeler's apartment. There were a number of things we didn't talk about, and after our coffee she went back to the room labeled "Ladies."

I took advantage of her absence to ask the bartender a question that had been worrying me for some time. He wasn't Pablo, but a younger man with rimless glasses and thin black hair. He looked more like a bank clerk than a bartender. I waylaid him at the end of the bar where nobody could hear me and I laid down a one-dollar bill and said, "How long has the lady been here? I mean, before I came?"

He plucked the bill from the bar and tucked it into a pocket of his white jacket with one smooth motion and answered me without looking up from squeezing a lemon for a whisky sour. "She was at the bar when I came on duty at seven o'clock, sir."

"Did she leave after that?"

"No, sir. She sat there until you came in."

"Is Guido here?"

"No, sir. He's gone for the evening." He dropped a cherry into the whisky sour, inserted a short straw with barber-pole stripes, and moved away.

I went back to the booth. The Venice Café was quite a place. Funny things happened here, and I didn't doubt that bartenders were often asked odd questions. Their answers, of course, depended upon whether or not their mothers had trained them always to tell the truth, or upon the amount of cash offered them to forget temporarily their mothers' training. I wondered if perhaps my lonely buck had been slightly niggardly. But *somebody* had squeezed a trigger zinging four .22 slugs at me. I shivered at the recollection.

Vivian Prosper came back and sat down. She had applied fresh make-up and had combed her hair until it shone. She was more attractive and alluring than any calendar girl ever painted. I said, "Want a brandy or something?"

She shook her head. "No, thanks. I'm tired of drinking, tired of everything."

I raised my eyebrows. "Everything?" I'm just an old roué at heart.

"Don't be crude," she said. "I mean that people drink too much, and they talk too much, and they rush around madly until they die. There must be more to life than that." She placed a cigarette between her lips and I held a match for her. She said abruptly, "Why did you open my purse and look at my gun?" and she blew smoke over my head.

Here it was. Why did I, indeed? I said carefully, "I wanted to be sure that you were carrying it. Keep carrying it, especially when you leave the house. There's a killer loose, remember? I'd feel better if I knew you had it."

Her expression softened. "Why, Andy," she said mockingly, "I didn't know you cared."

This was more like it, and I pushed things a little. Maybe a little too fast. "Let's go to my place. You don't have to drink—we'll just sit and talk."

She shook her head. "I don't think so, Andy. Not anymore. I—I don't feel right about it, and besides, I think Sergeant Navarre has a man following me. A huge dark man in a brown suit. I've seen him twice today."

That would be Kotz, I thought, one of Navarre's men, all right. I had to give Navarre credit. He must know now that Vivian had spent last night in my apartment, and yet, when I talked to him at Mrs. Koppus' house, he had discreetly refrained from mentioning it to me. He wasn't missing any tricks, and I reminded myself once more never to underestimate police intelligence.

"And," Vivian Prosper added, "I'm very tired. I think I'll go home and straight to bed."

"All right," I said. "Maybe when this is over you'll come and see me again."

"Maybe," she said carelessly. "Who knows?"

I paid the check and we went outside and stood under the night sky. Cars whizzed past on the highway and a soft breeze blew Vivian's hair across one cheek. She brushed back the hair, and smiled at me. "Thanks for the dinner, Andy." She moved away. "Good night."

"Hey," I said. "How about a lift? I came out in a taxi."

She hesitated for only an instant, then said, "Of course." I followed her to a pale grey Buick sedan.

We didn't talk much on the ride back into town. She drove swiftly and with skill and I just sat and let the soft air fan my face. Twice I made what I hoped were witty remarks in an attempt to recapture a little of whatever it was we'd had the night before, but it was no good. I may as well have been talking to a cool, casual acquaintance. She just didn't respond. I gave up and turned on the radio. A good band was playing Jelly Roll Morton's arrangement of "Sugar Foot Stomp" and I listened to it and smoked a cigarette and thought to hell with Vivian Prosper.

Once she said, "If you'd like a drink, there's a bottle in the glove compartment."

"No, thanks," I said shortly. A drink wouldn't help what was wrong with me. I had the Vivian Prosper blues, and there wasn't any cure for that except Vivian Prosper and maybe a repeat performance of the night before. After the events of the day, ending with the zing of bullets too close to my head, it may have been that I wanted to reassure myself about her, to try to dispel the nasty little barbs of suspicion that had been prodding me. It had been paradise, all right, or at least the nearest thing to paradise that a perfect physical meeting between a man and a woman can be, but now it was apparently paradise lost for me, the same as it had been for Allan Frederick Keeler. With Vivian in this kind of ice-cold mood, and with a panting little sister like Linda underfoot and begging for attention, I had to admit that I didn't blame Keeler too much for forgetting his marriage vows. But the sonofabitch had lied to me about not seeing Linda after his divorce from Vivian and I decided to talk to him about that.

Not that Keeler's lying meant anything, or that I blamed him for lying to me; it was just that I had figured him for a weak character who had cheated on his wife for no good reason. One of those cake-and-eat-it-too boys. But he had played it smart, had taken what he could get, was still taking it, apparently, and in a way he had the laugh on Vivian. I laughed silently to myself. Then I remembered the bullets smacking into

the bricks above my head and I shut off my inward
laughter.

I had the feeling that somewhere along the line I'd
missed the boat. The feeling had started when Vivian
told me about Navarre's man following her around. It
would be Kotz, all right. He was one of the biggest men
in the homicide division, a dark and powerful Arme-
nian, quiet, fast with a gun, and unshakable on a tailing job in spite of his size. I turned in the seat and gazed
out the rear window. There were a number of cars behind us, and any one of them could be Kotz's. What
did Navarre know that I didn't? The thought worried
me until the Buick stopped at the curb in front of my
apartment house.

I didn't try any last-ditch tactics. If she wasn't in
the mood, I wasn't going to get down on my knees and
plead with her, even though I suddenly knew that I'd
been anticipating this evening a lot more than I'd admitted to myself. But that's what comes from mixing
business with pleasure, especially such rich and exotic
pleasure as Vivian Prosper. Reluctantly I opened the
door of the Buick.

It was then that I saw Allan Frederick Keeler standing on the steps of the apartment building. He spotted
me and came over to the curb. It wasn't until he'd
peered into the Buick that he recognized Vivian, and
the look on his face was one of acute surprise, followed
by embarrassment.

Vivian said coolly, "Hello, Allan."

"Hello," he said stiffly. "How have you been?"

"Very well, Allan. And you?"

"Good enough, I guess. I—I've been waiting for
Mr. Brice." There was a small piece of adhesive tape
over the right side of his high poetic forehead, conceal-
ing the spot where the intruder in his apartment had
struck him. He was wearing a tan tweed jacket, the tan
gabardine slacks he'd had on when I found him
knocked silly behind the bed, and the green-dotted

bow tie was tied very neatly in the slot of his white shirt collar. He looked at me. "Could I speak with you for a moment?"

"Sure," I said, and he stood aside while I climbed out of the Buick. I lifted a hand to Vivian. "Thanks for the ride."

She gave me a stiff smile. "You're welcome." Her gaze shifted to Keeler and she said brightly, "It was nice seeing you, Allan."

He nodded his head and tried to smile, but it was a weak attempt. I closed the Buick's door and it pulled away from the curb with an excessive roar of power and headed up the street. Keeler watched it until it mingled with the lights and the traffic. There was a sad forlorn look on his face.

I said, "Buck up, pal." I thought I knew how he felt.

He gave me a wan smile and his silky mustache glinted yellowly in the light. "She's marvelous," he said. "Why did I ever let her get away from me?"

"We all make mistakes," I told him. "Water over the dam. What did you want to see me about?"

He spent a little time lighting a cigarette before he answered. I noticed that the hand holding a silver lighter trembled a little. He looked at me directly then and said, "The police came to see me this afternoon."

"Yeah, I know."

"You sent them?"

"No."

"Then I had a telephone call shortly after the police left. It was about this dead man in Linda's car—a strange voice, a man. All he said was 'Keep your nose out of the Prosper business or you'll get worse than a sore head.' Then he hung up." Keeler drew deeply on his cigarette and added, "I don't like that, Brice. I think somebody mixed up in the killing has been following you around, and your visit to my place has involved

me in it. I don't want any part of it. I no longer have
any connection with the Prosper family."

"Since when?" I asked him softly. "I hear you've
been seeing Linda."

His face twisted as if he were in pain. "Who says
I've been seeing her?"

"Vivian. Big Sister Vivian, your one-time wife. She
says. Damn you, you lied to me."

"How would she know?" he asked violently.
"She's lying to you, trying to implicate me. She's a
coldhearted, jealous, scheming bitch."

"Shut up," I snarled. "Shut the hell up." I had
heard all this before, and I didn't want to hear it again.
I didn't like to hear it even if it were true. I sneered at
Keeler, "But still you're nuts about her?"

"Yes, damn you, in spite of what she is. Why
should I waste my time with Linda? She caused me to
lose Vivian, and I'll never forgive her for that, do you
hear?"

"I hear," I said. "Calm down. If you aren't mixed
up in this, you have nothing to worry about."

"I'm going to ask for police protection," he said.
"They might do anything."

"Who's 'they'?"

"The person who killed that man—maybe the person who entered my apartment, or the one who telephoned me. How the hell do I know? You're a detective—why don't you get to work and clean up this
mess instead of driving around with Vivian? Just because I happened to have been married to her, you're
involving me in it, and I won't have it." His eyes were
wild and he began to tremble. "I demand police protection."

"All right. Relax. I'll ask Navarre if he can spare a
man, and let you know. Maybe not tonight, but the
first thing in the morning. O.K.?"

He seemed to have got a firmer grip on himself.
"Thanks, Brice," he said in a quieter voice. He took a

last deep drag on his cigarette and crushed it out on the sidewalk. "I—I don't want to seem like a—a coward, but this has got on my nerves."

I patted his arm. "Sure, I understand. You need a drink. Come up and I'll make you one."

He sighed deeply. "No, thanks. I'll be all right." He turned abruptly and walked away.

As I watched him go, I felt a little sorry for him. He'd had Vivian once, and Linda, too, but now he had nothing but memories and he was so scared that he could taste it. I decided that maybe it would be a good idea for Navarre to put a man on him, for Keeler's protection and as a check on the things that were happening to him, and I really didn't blame him for wanting police protection.

But who was lying about his seeing Linda after his divorce from Vivian? He or Vivian? I decided to question Vivian a little more closely about it.

It was nine o'clock on a Thursday evening in August.

Chapter Fourteen

The elevator was busy and I climbed the three flights to my apartment. As soon as I unlocked the door I saw the lights and I swung away from the door and froze with my back to the wall, leaving the door slightly ajar. I got my .32 in my hand and I waited maybe three seconds. The memory of the gay hum of bullets was still very much with me and I was jumpy as hell. So I stood there with my back against the wall and the gun in my hand, just like a character out of a mystery movie.

Nothing happened. No sound, no nothing, just the lights in my apartment, and I knew I'd turned them off when I left. I decided to go in before somebody came along the hall and saw me with the gun in my hand. There was no point in fooling around. I kicked the door open wide and moved in fast, the gun in front of me.

Linda Prosper said, "Hi, you."

I wiped sweat from my forehead, pocketed the gun, and closed the door. Then I turned to look at her. She was sitting on the divan with a glass in her hand, and a bottle of my bourbon was on the low table before her. She was wearing a light gray loose topcoat buttoned to her throat, and brown-and-white saddle oxfords. Her legs were bare, without even socks. Her dark curly hair had been combed back from her small oval face and tied in a bun behind with a red ribbon. She wore no make-up and her eyes were big and dark in her scrubbed-looking little girl's face.

I tossed my hat to a chair and said, "How did you get in?"

She waved the glass airily. "Easy. Nothing to it. I just told the elevator boy I was your sister come to visit you and he got a key and let me in. Easy."

"What else did you tell him?"

"Why, nothing." Her eyes were wide and innocent, "He was very nice about it. Was it wrong of him?"

"Oh, no," I said. "Not at all. He has standing instructions to always let brunettes into my apartment at any hour of the day or night."

"Blondes, too?" she asked slyly.

"Yeah, blondes, too. I'm hell with the women." Then I caught the implication of her question and I said, "What do you mean by that?"

"My sister, Vivian, is a blonde. Or hadn't you noticed?"

I changed the subject. "How did you get out of the house?"

She snapped her fingers. "Pooh. Easy as pie. I just put on some shoes and a coat, sneaked quiet like a mouse down the back stairs, scooted out to the street behind the hedge, grabbed a taxi—and here I am." She spread her arms to show me that she was here. Some of her drink spilled to the divan.

"There's supposed to be three cops watching you," I said.

She giggled slyly. "I know it. I fooled 'em." She took a swallow of her drink and I wondered uneasily how much of the bourbon she'd soaked up before I arrived. Plenty, I guessed, at least plenty for a seventeen-year-old.

I retrieved my hat from the chair and moved over to her. "Come on, honey. I'll take you home."

She shook her head violently. "Don't wanna go home. Gonna stay here with you, like Vivian did last night. Won't that be fun? Only I'll be more fun than Vivian. You'll see." She pointed a small finger at me. "You just wait and see."

I was shocked. Maybe I shouldn't have been, knowing what I did about her bedroom conduct, but still I was shocked. I said cautiously, "Why do you say that Vivian was here?"

She giggled. "I can always tell when Vivian has a new love. When she comes in from being with a man she likes she always hums 'Jingle Bells' while she's getting undressed in her room. Only she was gone all night last night and when she came in this morning she hummed it while she was changing clothes. She didn't go to bed and I knew that she must have slept *someplace*." She paused and added with a bright glint in her eyes, "Anyhow, she must have slept a *little*. And you're her newest boy friend, and I figured it out that she was here with you."

I tried to look dignified. "I'm not her boy friend, and she wasn't here."

She laughed and lifted her glass with both hands and drained it like a kid drinking milk. Then she stood up and moved close to me. I backed away, but she kept moving in, her head down, and giving me a shy up-from-under look. "You're just being noble," she said softly. "You don't have to protect Vivian. I don't care what she does. I just want to show you that I'm nicer than Vivian. Lots, lots nicer." She pressed her forehead against me and I saw the soft fuzz of dark hair at the base of her neck.

I knew my duty and I wanted to do it. But it was slightly disconcerting, after my frustrating evening with Vivian, to come home to a luscious little armful like Linda. Nevertheless, I was firm. Besides, I was already too much involved with the Prosper family. I pushed her away from me, perhaps a little reluctantly, and I crossed to the telephone with the resolute intention of calling Navarre and telling him to have his men come and get her.

But Linda was ahead of me. With a gay little laugh she scurried past me to the phone and I saw her hands working with the buttons of the topcoat. I tried to reach around her for the phone, but she pushed my arms away and said poutingly, "Don't be an old meanie. Let's have fun."

I'd had enough. "Get away from that goddamned phone," I snarled, and I picked her up and carried her to the divan and dumped her down. The topcoat fell away from her then and with eye-popping clarity I saw that beneath it she was wearing nothing but an extremely sheer black nylon nightgown.

For a second it unnerved me. Then I set my jaw in the approved true-blue hero manner and attempted to button the coat, but she giggled and squirmed away from me. She was like a snake and I couldn't hold her and I found myself holding the empty coat. As she tripped lightly across the room I saw that the hem of the nightgown had been pinned up so that it wouldn't show beneath the coat. And she was wise enough in feminine wiles to kick off the saddle oxfords; she was well aware of the incongruity and grotesqueness of scuffed saddle oxfords on her feet in contrast to her curving little pink and white body gauzily clad in sheer black.

She posed on her toes, like a ballet dancer, and spread her arms gracefully. "Aren't I lovely?" she cried. "Don't you like me? Better than Vivian?"

I stood helplessly. She was truly a lovely sight. The nightgown left nothing to my imagination and I decided that she was a miniature copy of her sister's long-legged beauty.

"Vivian locked up all my dresses," she said. "But I'm too smart for her. Don't you think this gown is nice?" She pirouetted like a fashion model. "It's a present from Arthur."

I found my voice. "Why don't you marry Arthur?"

"I will—someday. Vivian doesn't like him, but she's just jealous." She snapped her fingers. "Hell with Vivian. She never wants me to have any fun." She began to saunter slowly toward me, her hands clasped before her, her head tilted to one side. "Don't you want to have fun?"

1 was worried and irritated. And tempted. I admit it. I told myself that Linda Prosper was an oversexed, underaged delinquent. To trifle with her would be playing with the hottest kind of fire—or would it? She stood very close to me and I didn't back away.

She counted on three fingers. "Your name is Andrew Brice, you're a detective, and Vivian hired you to work for her."

"Who said?"

"Jerome. He's really quite nice. Vivian quarrels with him, but he likes me. He isn't really my father, you know."

"Yes, I know," I said, remembering Vivian's remark concerning Jerome's and Linda's love-making in the garage. "Tell me why you came here."

For just an instant I thought I detected a hint of fear in her eyes. Then she said, "I want to know what you have found out about what happened to me. How that—that man got in my car."

"Don't you know?" I asked, amazed. She looked sincere, and she sounded sincere.

She lowered her gaze and fingered a button on my shirt. "I know a—a little. The beginning, anyhow. If I tell you, will you be nice to me?"

I didn't have any choice. It was my duty and my obligation to do everything necessary to learn who had killed Steve Lapham, and why. It made everything simple and clear cut. I had tried to be true to Vivian, but now it was out of my hands. Maybe I was a little too eager, but what's wrong about enjoying your work? I put my arms around her and instantly she pressed against me with a little sigh. She smelled cleanly of soap and there was a faint perfume in her hair.

"Sure, honey," I told her, "I'll be as nice as you want. Now just tell me all about it. How did he get in your car? Who killed him? Why did you marry him, anyhow? Who was with you at the Venice Café?"

She moved against me, snuggling even closer, and her hands slid up beneath my coat and gently caressed my back. "Be nice to me first," she said in a muffled voice.

I tilted her head back and bent to kiss her. Her small mouth met mine hungrily and her lips were soft and hot and they clung in a way that no seventeen-year-old's ever should.

At last I pushed her gently away from me.

"No, no," she said breathlessly, clinging to me. "Kiss me some more."

"Will you tell me about what happened?"

"Yes, yes."

So I kissed her some more. Beneath my hands the nylon moved over her small smooth body and it was just about the nicest work I ever had. It was work I hated to leave, but I did, eventually. I pulled her arms down and held her at a comparatively safe distance. "Now tell me," I pleaded.

She strained toward me. "More," she whispered.

"Don't you worry," I promised. "There'll be more. Just tell me who you were with at the Venice Café—the other man, not Lapham—and what happened. Then I'll really be nice to you."

She couldn't stand still. "All right, I will, I will. Let's have fun first."

"No," I said stonily. I was really proud of myself.

Abruptly she stopped squirming and stood quietly. When I thought it was safe, I dropped my hands from her arms. Still she didn't move and I breathed a sigh of relief. "All right," she said with downcast eyes. "You win."

"And just in time," I muttered to myself.

She looked quickly up at me. "What?"

"Never mind," I said. "Just tell me."

"I intend to tell you," she said primly, "but first you must tell me what you have found out and how much Vivian knows."

Inside of me something seemed to snap, like the first strand of a rope stretched to the breaking point. I grabbed her small round shoulders and I shook her and I shouted at her. "Damn it, you tell me, and then I'll tell you, and then we can both be nice to each other. O.K., for God's sake?"

She laughed in my face. "You're cute when you're mad," she said.

"You going to tell me?" I was ready to slug her.

"Will you make me a drink first?"

"No!"

She twisted gracefully away from me and posed for a second in the middle of the room, her gaze on my face. Then she stretched luxuriously and contentedly with a body motion that would have been the envy of any top-billed burlesque teaser. The sheer black nylon slid and shimmered and caressed her. "Don't you think I have a lovely body?" she murmured.

I could feel, deep inside of me, the remaining rope strands snapping and I swung away from her. A man could stand just so much. To hell with the whole goddamned Prosper family, and Jerome Pitt, and the dog, too, if they had a dog. The thing for me to do was to get her the hell out of my apartment, as soon as possible. I strode to the divan, grabbed her topcoat, and turned with it in my hands. Then I stood petrified at what I saw.

She had slipped off the nightgown. It lay in a filmy little heap at her bare feet. It hadn't concealed very much when she'd been wearing it, but now nothing was concealed. She stood with her hands behind her, one knee turned gracefully in, her eyes downcast.

"May I have a cigarette?" she murmured.

That did it. The last strand of the rope had snapped. I was suddenly cool and calm. The nightgown, flimsy as it was, had made her seem more mature, more desirable than she really was. Now she was just a naked kid, a child, really, just playing games, and all I wanted to do was to cover her up and get her back home where she belonged. I advanced toward her, holding the coat in front of me, like a man trying to catch an escaped canary. She laughed gaily, danced away, and found refuge behind a floor lamp in a far corner. Grimly I stalked her.

The door opened and Vivian Prosper stepped into my living room.

I was speechless, horrified. I stood frozen, holding the coat, staring at Vivian dumbly. But she ignored me, her eyes on Linda. She was still wearing the lime-green dress and carrying the basket purse. For one horrible ice-filled moment no one spoke.

Then Linda, from her corner behind the floor lamp where I'd hoped to corral her, said nervously, "Well, I'll be darned, if it isn't my sweet big sister."

Vivian's gaze swept the room. She spotted the nightgown on the floor, picked it up, and tossed it to Linda. "Put that on," she said coldly. Without looking at me she took the coat from my numb fingers and advanced toward her sister. "Come on. I'm taking you home."

As Linda wiggled into the nightgown she said poutingly, "Don't wanna go home."

"Be quiet," Vivian snapped. She draped the coat over Linda's shoulders and turned to me. "How did she get away from the police?" she asked.

I started to speak, but no words came out. I tried again. "Uh—she didn't get away from the police. Wait here a minute." I hurried to the door and went out. I was glad to get out.

Down on the street I spotted Jake Lindsey, one of Navarre's men, camped on the sidewalk opposite the front door of the apartment building. He was chewing on a cigar and trying to look like a man waiting for a bus. He even had a newspaper under his arm. He saw me come out, but he pretended not to notice. I went up to him and said, "You can come up and get her now, Jake."

He turned to me with a fake look of surprise. "Why, hello, Andy!"

"Stop hamming it up. Did Navarre tell you to let her skip, if she tried, and then follow her?"

He grinned at me. "Yep, that's right. He figured she might lead us to something. But she didn't—just to you." He punched my ribs with an elbow. "How was it, boy?"

"I wouldn't know."

He guffawed loudly.

I looked around, but I didn't see anything of Kotz. I said, "Has Navarre got a man on the older sister, too?"

"He had Kotz tailing her for a while, but I think he took him off. She ain't bad, either." He leaned toward me and said confidentially, "Say, Andy, I got a bet with Deegan—he's in the alley covering the back door. Navarre told us that the older sister locked up the young one's clothes. What's she got on under that coat? Just panties? Deegan says she's bare, but I say panties and maybe a bra. Who wins?"

"You both lose," I told him. "Come on up and get her."

I turned and went slowly back up the stairs to my apartment. It was like the last mile to the death chamber. When I entered the living room Linda was huddled on the divan with tears on her face. The coat was buttoned tightly around her. Vivian sat stiffly on a chair. I said to her, "The police followed her here. They'll be up to take her home."

"Thank you," she said.

"You're welcome," I replied politely. I went into the kitchen and closed the door.

I remembered the Martinis I'd made in anticipation of Vivian's visit and I took the pitcher out of the refrigerator and filled a glass. It tasted good and I ate one of the shrimps I'd fixed. It tasted good too and I had another. From the living room I heard voices and a door slammed. Then silence. I poured more Martini, doused another shrimp in the sauce, and wondered if I was still working for Vivian. But I didn't worry about it—not too much. The morning would be soon enough to find out. I'd been through enough for one night, I thought, and I began to feel a little sorry for myself.

The door opened and Vivian Prosper stepped into the kitchen. She smiled and nodded at the Martini and shrimp. "May I have some of that?"

"Are you still speaking to me?" I stood up, holding a glass in one hand and a shrimp on a toothpick in the other.

"Of course. Why not?"

I pointed the shrimp at the living room. "B—but …" She moved up close and patted my cheek. "You don't have to explain. I was listening outside at the door. I'm proud of you. Linda can be very—provocative."

"Provocative?" I blurted. "Listen—"

She placed her fingers over my mouth. "Shush, I know. It's all right. Did she give you a bad time?"

I grinned at her. "Kind of, maybe—for a while there." I felt suddenly happy. Virtue always pays.

Vivian sat down at the kitchen table and we finished the Martinis and the shrimp and everything was wonderful.

Chapter Fifteen

I don't have a television set but I have a good record player and a cabinet of records. No Chopin and Debussy, as Jacqueline Hart of Midstate University had so fondly imagined; just a collection that I like and play when I'm in the mood. Some classics and a few of the modern composers, but mostly old popular tunes that carry me back to my high-school and early college days, the happiest time in anyone's life, a time before things get serious and before you find out that the world doesn't play for matches and that it's dog eat dog and to hell with your neighbor.

Vivian liked "I Can't Get Started with You" and I let it play over and over while we sat on the divan with the lights low. We talked in low tones with the music a soft background in the shadows and our cigarettes glowed in the semidarkness. I told her how I'd heard Bunny Berigan play in Toledo a short time before he died and twice I made tall drinks with a lot of ice and soda and very little bourbon and I was at peace with the world.

Vivian touched my hand. "I like you, Andy."

"Why?"

"Because we like the same things ... and because the way you handled Linda tonight." She laughed softly. "You've had a bad evening, haven't you?"

"It's fine now," I said.

"I'm sorry that I was so—so cool to you during dinner. Will you forgive me?"

"Sure," I said. I was in a mellow forgiving mood. "Forget it."

"It wasn't you. It's just that I've been so worried about Linda and her connection with this awful business. And when I suspected that the police had a man observing my movements, well, I thought it best not to be seen coming here. But I don't care now."

"To hell with the police," I said. "It's none of their business. If you don't care, I don't. Anyhow, I think Navarre decided that it was a waste of time to keep a man on your trail and took him off."

"Did Linda tell you anything?"

I shook my head. "Nothing. I tried, and she about drove me nuts, but she didn't tell me a damn thing."

She sighed. "I know. She's a strange girl. She has a—a complex of some kind. She's always seemed to resent me and she's very stubborn. Why did Allan want to see you? And what happened to his head?"

Earlier in the evening I'd been expecting her to ask me about Keeler, but I'd forgotten it and now her question surprised me. I said carefully, "I talked to him yesterday afternoon. I thought maybe he could give me a line on some of Linda's friends, some that maybe you wouldn't know about. Just before I got there somebody who had been snooping around his apartment slugged him on the head, and—"

"Burglars, or what?" she asked quickly.

"I don't know, and he didn't get a look at whoever it was. Anyhow, he told me that he hadn't seen Linda since you divorced him."

"He's lying," she said evenly. "Linda told me that she'd been seeing him."

"Somebody's lying," I said. "Linda or Keeler or—you."

"Do you think I'm lying?" There was a faint edge to her voice.

I smiled at her. "You wouldn't lie to me, would you?"

"You know I wouldn't. Why should I?" She moved until she was close beside me.

"Anyhow," I said, "Keeler came to see me because he's scared. He had a threatening phone call, and he wants police protection. He blames me for involving him in the trouble."

"Poor Allan," she said. "He hasn't much courage." She placed her glass on the table and leaned back against me. Her hair brushed my cheek and her thigh was warm against mine. "Let's forget other people," she whispered, "Let's think of just us."

I put my own glass on the table and turned to her and pulled her down on the divan and stretched out beside her. Her eyes were closed and she didn't speak and I felt her tremble a little. I held her close and I

kissed her and presently the trembling stopped and her
lips grew warm and urgently clinging.

A little later my phone began to ring. I let it ring
and at last it stopped.

At midnight I sat by the radio smoking a cigarette
and listening to the late news broadcast. Vivian was in
the bathroom and I was trying to decide whether I
wanted some coffee when I remembered the ringing of
the phone. At precisely the moment I remembered, it
rang again. It was one of those things that makes you
wonder about the phenomenon known as telepathy.

When I lifted the receiver and said, "Hello," I
didn't recognize the slow, thin, deliberate answering
voice.

"Mr. Brice?"

"Yes."

"This is Dr. Otten. I attended you yesterday afternoon at the Venice Café."

"Oh, yes." Yesterday afternoon seemed like a long
time ago. "I got your message and I called you twice,
but I guess you were out. How are you, Doctor?"

"Very well, thank you. Yes, I've been away from
my office. House calls, you know." He paused, and I
heard him cough. Then a kind of gurgling sound came
over the wire and I wondered if he were gargling
mouthwash or taking a drink from a bottle. I decided
on the latter, and I waited. Presently he said, "Mr.
Brice, are you there?"

"I'm here, Doctor."

"Mr. Brice, it occurred to me that perhaps I'd better
inform you that I took the liberty of doing an analysis
of the contents of the stomach pump I used on you
yesterday. I hope you don't mind."

I suppressed a gulp before I said, "I don't mind,
Doctor, but why?"

"Mr. Brice, I will be quite frank. When I was treating you I noticed a dilated condition of your pupils and

I suspected the presence of a narcotic." He stopped talking and I heard the gurgling sound again. Then he said, "Mr. Brice, are you there?"

"Still here. What're you drinking—bourbon?"

"Gin, sir. I always drink gin. Will you join me? Oh, stupid of me. We are conversing on the telephone, aren't we?"

"That's right, Doctor. I'm not in your office. So you found the presence of a narcotic?"

"Yes, I did. How are you feeling, sir?"

"Fine."

"You are very fortunate. Apparently only a small amount entered your system before I applied the stomach pump."

"A small amount of what?"

"Atropine, Mr. Brice. Sometimes called belladonna, or deadly nightshade. A truly deadly poison. It is used medically in minute doses as an antispasmodic—infants with colic, you know?—as a sedative, and in the treatment and examination of the eyes." He paused to take another swig of the gin, a short one this time, and when he spoke again his voice was very clear and precise. "Are you there, Mr. Brice?"

"Yep."

"Good. What was I saying?"

"You were telling me about a drug called atropine."

"Oh, yes. Thank you, sir. You must understand that in its several forms there are certain toxic and pharmaceutical differences, but in sufficient quantity atropine in any of its forms can cause death. You had in your stomach a sufficient quantity, sir."

I swallowed. "Uh—that is very interesting, Doctor. I certainly appreciate your telling me."

"You are very welcome." He paused again, but the gurgle didn't come and I wondered if his bottle was empty. Then he coughed delicately and said. "Mr.

Brice, you weren't attempting anything—ah—foolish, were you?"

I didn't feel like laughing, but I managed a kind of cackle. "You mean suicide? Oh, no, nothing like that, Doctor."

"I am very glad to hear you say that, sir. You did not appear to be the neurotic suicide type."

"Thank you, Doctor."

"Then, Mr. Brice," he said carefully and precisely, "am I to assume that you took the atropine inadvertently?"

"No," I said, "you are not to assume that."

"You realize that the only other alternative is that it was placed in your food or drink without your knowledge? Am I to assume that?"

"You have me there, Doctor. Thanks for calling me."

"Just a moment, Mr. Brice, please. Are you there?"

"Yes," I said wearily.

"Good. There is something else in which you may be interested. While I was treating you I heard the waitress—Blanche is her name, I believe—tell Guido, the proprietor, that you had asked her about two men and a girl who had been in the café the previous evening. Does that interest you?"

"Very much, Doctor." I realized that my fingers had tightened on the receiver.

"Well, sir, it just happens that I was in the café that evening. In fact, now that I think of it, I am in the café almost every evening. I noticed a small dark girl in the company of two men and I could describe them to you. In fact, Mr. Brice, I talked to one of the men later in the evening and I could tell you his name, if you wished."

I leaned forward in the chair. I said, "Tell me."

Vivian Prosper came out of the bathroom and looked at me curiously. I held a finger to my lips. She lit a cigarette and sat down on the divan.

Dr. Otten's delicate cough came over the wire and I heard him sigh like the tired, boozed-up old man he was. "Mr. Brice, I have practiced medicine and surgery for forty years—no, let me think—forty-four years, and I am fully aware of my obligation to my patients. However, what I have to tell you now does not concern your health, and I wonder if private investigators come by needed information as easily as that."

"As easily as what?"

"By merely wishing."

"How do you know I'm a private investigator?"

He coughed once more. "Your wallet fell from your coat. I—ah—happened to see your license card."

I thought, Fell out, hell. You took it out of my pocket and peeked. But I was kind of glad. It put me on familiar round. "All right, Doc," I said, "how much?" It wasn't until after I'd said it that I realized I'd shortened the "Doctor" to "Doc."

He caught the change in my manner and he said in a hurt voice, "Now, Mr. Brice, I *did* provide you with professional service yesterday afternoon. You would probably have died, you know." He paused and I guessed that he was gazing sadly at his empty bottle. Then he said, "I think fifty dollars would cover it."

"Twenty-five," I said.

"That will be satisfactory, Mr. Brice," he said quickly, and I wished I'd offered him ten.

"Fine," I said, "now give me the man's name."

"Would that be discreet, Mr. Brice? The telephone, you know...."

He wanted his twenty-five dollars before he talked and I didn't blame him. "Where do you live?" I asked him.

He gave me an address on Ridge Road, south of town and not far from the Venice Café. I wrote it down and said, "I'll be out. I'm leaving now."

"Very good, Mr. Brice," he said quietly, and hung up.

Vivian looked a question at me and I said, "I'm going out to see a man on Ridge Road. Want to come along?"

"Who? What man?"

"An old doctor named Otten. He used a stomach pump on me yesterday and probably saved me from dying of poisoning. He was at the Venice Café when Linda was there with the two men, and he's going to give me the name of the second man. We know that one of them was Lapham."

"Poisoning?" she asked, her eyes big.

"All in the line of duty. I'll tell you about it sometime. Coming?"

"You *have* been working, haven't you?"

"You're paying me, aren't you?"

She stood up. "I intend to pay you—when you present me with a bill. Did someone try to poison you? Really?"

"Really." I grinned at her. "Don't worry, you'll get a bill."

"Whatever the amount, it'll be a bargain," she said. "But who—"

"Never mind." I put on my coat, took the .32 from the inside pocket, and checked the clip.

She said soberly, "Guns tonight?"

"Just standard equipment after midnight. Let's go."

"You're sure you want me along?"

I pulled her to me and kissed her. "I'll always want you." I meant it, too. "This is it—the pay-off, the windup, the finish. When I know that man's name I'll know the killer."

She leaned back in my arms and placed her fingers over my lips. "I'll go with you, Andy," she whispered, "but promise you'll always want me—no matter what?"

"Sure," I said. It was an easy promise to make. She was sugar and spice and everything nice, and champagne and caviar to boot.

"I love you, Andy," she said softly. "I'm afraid I love you." She kissed me long and hard and then she pushed away from me and moved to the door. "Ready?" she said brightly. There were sudden tears in her eyes.

In the hall I said, "Wait down in front. I'll get my car from the garage."

"We can go in mine."

I hesitated only a second before I said carelessly, "O.K."

I steered her down the stairs. I didn't want the elevator boy to be making cracks at me, as was his habit. Vivian's Buick was across the street about halfway down the block. We walked to it and she got behind the wheel without asking me to drive. I was content to sit beside her and let the night breeze hit my face. At the first traffic light she said, "You call the turns."

"Go to the Venice Café. I'll tell you from there."

We cut across town to the lake boulevard and presently the lights of the city were below us. There was half of a moon peeking from behind dark moving clouds, and far out over the lake, toward the Canadian shore, the sky was a dead black. Once the boulevard dipped almost to the beach and I had a glimpse of white foam breaking over dark sand. The boats in the yacht basin were tossing at their moorings and sea gulls were swirling around a yellow dock light like moths flirting with a candle. As we climbed the long four-lane ramp beyond the yacht basin the breeze grew suddenly damp and cool. The lights of the city were slipping away behind us and we were in a suburban section now and passing dark homes surrounded by trees and an occasional house with lights still burning. Below us on the far side of the highway the lake was black and glinting roughly in the streaked moonbeams, and once, when we slowed for a curve around a rocky jutting point, I heard the slap and roar of the wind-driven waters against the breakwater.

"Rain coming," I said.

"Good," Vivian said. "I like the rain, don't you?"

"Yes, if I'm near a fireplace with a drink in my hand, and if I'm not too lonely."

"Lonely now?"

I turned toward her and placed my hand on her thigh. Her skin was soft and warm beneath the thin dress, and with startling suddenness I wished I had her back in my apartment. She must have sensed what I felt, and I guess she felt it too, because she said in a throaty voice, "We've got something, haven't we? Something wonderful, that just the two of us know about."

"Yes," I said, and I looked up at her. But her gaze was on the road ahead and I saw her clean profile and her tawny hair blowing back from her face. "Are you coming back with me tonight?"

She shot me a quick glance. "Do you want me?"

"Bad," I said, and in the gloom and the wind my hand moved upward across the back of the seat to rest upon the nape of her neck. She kept her hands on the wheel and she stared straight ahead, but I could feel the quickening of her breathing.

She raised a hand from the wheel and placed it over my wrist. "Don't, you fool. I'm driving."

"Stop driving," I said.

Instantly the Buick slowed. "All right. Where?" she asked.

"Up ahead. I'll tell you."

"You've been there before?"

"Yes, but not lately."

"Who was she? I hate her."

The rain hit us then, cold and stinging, straight off the lake; and we rolled up the windows. Now we were in a little moving house, cozy and alone with the storm outside. The hum of the motor was a faraway sound. The windshield wipers swished gently and the road ahead looked wet and black and the rain danced and jumped in the glare of the headlights.

The hands of the clock on the dash pointed to a quarter of one in the morning. Suddenly, from out of nowhere, a cold uneasy feeling hit me and I wanted to hurry. There was plenty of time to be with Vivian after the night was over, and now wasn't the time for anything except getting to Dr. Otten's house as quickly as possible. We were on a wide stretch of highway and a car passed us, going fast, and the spray from its tires momentarily misted the windshield and mingled with the driving rain. As I watched the red taillights disappear in the darkness I remembered Dr. Otten's dry, precise, drunken voice: "In fact, Mr. Brice, I talked to one of the men later in the evening and I could tell you his name, if you wished."

Vivian said, "Don't tell me, then."

"Don't tell you what?"

"Who the girl was—the one you were with at this place, where you parked with her. I don't want to know, I don't care. She's in your past, gone and forgotten, isn't she? Isn't she, Andy?"

I moved away from her. "Sure," I said. "Long ago." I placed two cigarettes in my mouth, lit them, and handed one to her.

She took it, said, "Thanks, darling. Where is this place where we can stop?"

That damn "darling" again. Why did I resent it now? She had a right to call me darling if she wanted to. "We've passed it," I said.

The Buick faltered for a second and she said reproachfully, "Why didn't you tell me?"

"The rain started and I missed it."

"Oh." We gathered speed again.

I said, "I haven't any more steak, but we can have ham and eggs for breakfast." I thought of the things

I'd bought for Blanche Dorinda Swickert, and I added, "Or hamburger, pickles, potato chips, and rye."

She shot me a quick smile. "Is this an invitation or a proposition?"

"A friendly invitation."

"Platonic?"

"No, I'm afraid it isn't a platonic invitation."

"Good," she laughed, and she patted my knee. "Can I sleep until noon?"

"You can sleep all day." I peered through the rain and saw the lights of the Venice Café. "Turn left at the next road."

Chapter Sixteen

I had an uneasy feeling that I should have called Navarre, but it was too late now and I could call him after I talked to Dr. Otten. We drove back and forth twice in the rain on Ridge Road before I spotted the place. It was a small frame house back off the road with no other houses near it. We were in a semi-developed section in rolling land with a scattering of woods and thickets. On our first run down the road I missed it, and after we turned around and came back I might have missed it again if the headlights hadn't caught the dull glint of a faded gilt-and-black sign stuck into the uncut grass of the front yard. "L. M. Otten, M.D." Yellow light streamed out over a small front porch and across the brick sidewalk leading up from the road.

"Here it is," I said to Vivian.

She pulled the Buick off the road, turned off the lights and the motor. I touched her shoulder. "Want to come in with me?"

I felt her shiver, faintly. "No, I—I don't think so."

"What's the matter?"

She turned toward me. Her face was a pale oval, her eyes dark shadows. "I'm scared."

"Of what?"

"Of what you may learn in there." She nodded at the house. "I mean, about Linda's part in that—that killing. She's just a kid, my little sister, and I feel as if somehow I've failed her, and Mother, too. I've tried, but I can't get close to her. She's wild, but a lot of young girls are wild, and they get over it. Sometimes I wonder if she's—she's normal. She does such crazy things. Like tonight—her sneaking out to come and see you. And marrying that boy. What's his name? Lapham?"

I nodded. "Steve."

"Why would she do a thing like that? She didn't care about him. And now this trouble." Her voice broke. "What can I do with her?"

"There are places you can put her," I said. "I know of a couple. One is the Calvert Home for Wayward Girls. It's private and—"

"No, no, I couldn't do that. It would kill her."

"Not Linda. She'd get along."

"But it wouldn't do any good. It would just restrain her until she got out."

"You might try a good psychiatrist, or a psychoanalyst," I told her.

"I did, once," she said bitterly, "but after she'd been going to him for some time I found out that she was meeting him between office sessions at a lodge up on the beach. He was married and had three children."

I was watching the house and it seemed to me that a shadow had moved across the light from the doorway. Dr. Otten was probably getting impatient. As I put my hand on the door latch it occurred to me that it was very possible that what the doctor had to tell me might put Linda in a place where her sister would not have to worry about her for a long time. In the poky you don't get boozed up and tear down to Kentucky and marry college boys, or go to bed with your sister's husband, or come home in the middle of the morning drunk and doped and with a dead man in your car, or chase after your sister's men friends by sneaking out of the house in a topcoat and nightgown, or race about in a Rolls-Royce with a dark man from God knows where, or go out with a pilot from Texas, or ride in jalopies with unidentified boys with crew haircuts, or make love in a garage with your stepfather, or keep secret trysts in a lodge on the beach with a middle-aged psychiatrist, a man professionally trained to help banish the kind of impulses that made a teen-ager keep secret trysts with middle-aged psychiatrists in a lodge on the beach.

It was too much for me and I opened the car door. "I'll make it as quick as I can."

She leaned across me, opened the glove compartment, and took out a flat pint bottle. As she unscrewed the cap she said, "Mind if I have a drink while I wait? I seem to be slightly jittery. I feel like screaming long and loud."

"You never scream," I reminded her. "Remember?"

"It might help, even if it is a sign of female weakness."

I slid my arm around her and tilted her face upward with my left hand. She lay still in the crook of my arm, her eyes glinting green in the faint light. "I can take care of those jitters," I said.

"I'm counting on it," she whispered. Her lips parted and I kissed her and let her go.

She offered me the bottle. "Drink first?"

I shook my head. "Later."

As I pushed open the door she said, "Hurry, Andy," and then I was running through the rain up the brick walk to the porch.

The screen door had holes in it. The inner door was standing open and I saw a big marble fireplace with a Chinese-designed fire screen. Straight wooden chairs sat around the walls. A heavy squat oak table in the center of the room bore a disordered pile of ragged and torn magazines. The floor was covered with worn and rippling brown linoleum. Beyond the fireplace a door opened into a dark room, and above the mantel was a printed card that read:

The Doctor is IN
Please Be Seated

I opened the screen door and stepped inside. On my right another door led into a room that apparently was the office. There was a light there, too, and I saw the end of a glass-doored instrument cabinet, part of a shelf of books, an old-fashioned roll-top desk cluttered with papers. There was a telephone nestled in the piled papers and beside it sat an empty pint bottle with a gin label. I stood still, looking and listening. All I saw was the empty room and all I heard was the steady beat of the rain on the windows.

I said loudly, "Dr. Otten."

No answer, no sound. Only the rain and the far-off rumble of thunder. The rain came down harder, spattering and driving on the roof and on the porch beyond the screen door behind me. It was hot and close in Dr. Otten's waiting room and I could almost taste the smell of old leather and mold and dust, the bitter odor of medicines and drugs. There was another smell, too, a sweetish clinging smell not unfamiliar to me, and I called, "Dr. Otten," again, but in a small forlorn voice now, like the cry of a lost child wailing his loneliness and his fear in a dark wood at midnight.

Nothing but silence and the rain and the diminishing roll of thunder. I moved to the office and stood with my hand on the doorframe. I could see most of it now, and the special sweet smell hung cloying and heavy in the still air. The glass case was filled with an assortment of scissors, scalpels, forceps, and rolls of tape and gauze in various widths. Shelves on the opposite wall were filled with jars of pills and capsules and bottles containing varicolored liquids.

Directly before me was a high, narrow, leather-covered table with buckled straps at each end to control the possible spasmodic movements of patients being cut, probed, swabbed, stitched, or otherwise molested. The legs of the table were steel, ending in small rubber-tired wheels. A sheet was folded across the table, and when my gaze hit it I knew where the sweetish smell had come from. No doubt the sheet had once been white and crisp, but now it was almost completely soaked with fresh blood. It had flowed thickly over the edge of the table, and three silky strands hung as delicately as the filaments of a red spider web.

I moved slowly through the door of the office, not wanting to see what I knew I was going to see. He was on the floor on the far side of the table, between the table and the wall, and he lay peacefully on his side with his knees drawn up and his thin old hands clasped in an attitude of supplication. The short shaved hair glinted dully in the light and his lined, tired face was gray and sad and waxy with the nearness of death. There was blood on the floor beside him, welling thickly from the bubbling pool that was his chest.

I moved around the table and knelt beside him. "Dr. Otten," I said gently. "This is Brice. Can you hear me?" I felt the big vein beneath his jaw and the pulse was almost gone. There was nothing to do to help him. His tired old eyes were glazing and he was on the threshold of the Big Dark; but, still, in his eyes there was a faraway end-of-the-tunnel flicker of recognition, like the feeble last sputtering of a burned-out candle. His thin purple-flecked lips moved, and I leaned closer, ignoring the fact that my hand was resting in a shallow pool of his cooling blood. But all I heard was the ragged sound of his breathing and the sibilant whispers that might have been words.

"Louder," I pleaded. "Louder, please." I leaned over him until my ear was almost touching his lips.

I heard them then, the words, barely heard the slow, whispered, tortured words that almost faded before they reached my ear.

"He did it. Same man saw at Venice Café ... with girl called Linda ... and man named Steve.... They left, all three.... He came back.... Talked to him...." The voice died and the eyes stared blankly and the lips moved just a little.

"His name," I pleaded, and I shook him a little. "You said you knew it. Who?" I crouched over him and I felt the sweat on my forehead.

It seemed as if I waited a long time, but at last his lips moved slowly and with great effort. The old eyes rolled upward at me, imploringly, and one hoarse word came out: "Spotwood." And then abruptly, as if there had been a drawn curtain, the eyes went dead and dull, and the thin lips moved and worked and fell open and stayed open and the whole body went still.

I remained crouching over him for a minute, but his eyes bothered me; it seemed that even in death there was reproach in them, and I looked away and pushed myself slowly to my feet.

Vivian Prosper was standing in the office doorway and staring with wide eyes at what lay at my feet. Then her gaze shifted to me and she asked a silent white-faced question.

"Yes," I said heavily, "he's dead."

She swayed a little and lifted a hand to the doorframe. Her eyes shut and there was a tight white look around her mouth. I moved over and placed a hand on her arm. She opened her eyes, shook off my hand impatiently. "I—I'm all right," she said in an unsteady voice.

"Good girl," I said. "No screams, no hysterics." I left her and moved to the phone on the desk.

Behind me Vivian said quietly, "Who killed him? Do you know?"

I turned to face her. "Yes, I know. You'll be pleased. The poor old guy told me with his last breath. Arthur Spotwood killed him."

We stared at each other for maybe three seconds. Then she said in a faltering voice, "A-Arthur?"

"That's what you want, isn't it?" I said harshly. "He'll never marry Linda now—not when he's in the death house."

She was fighting it, pulling herself together. "I don't like Arthur," she said, and her voice was steady. "I don't trust him, and I don't want him to marry Linda. But why would he do a—a thing like that?" Her gaze roved to the dead man, and skittered away.

"To cover up," I said bitterly. "To keep him from talking. I'm not very happy about it. If I'd been smarter, Otten would be making his calls tomorrow and getting harmlessly drunk in the Venice Café tomorrow night, or maybe saving some no-good bastard's life, like he did mine, with his skill and his knowledge and a stomach pump. Spotwood has been on the prowl, watching me, following me. Once he tried to kill me with poison, and once with bullets. Tonight he knew we were headed for Dr. Otten's house and he overtook us and beat us here, and he killed him, to keep him from talking. He killed Steve Lapham, too, out of jealousy, and because he was married to Linda."

I stopped talking, and I was surprised to discover that I was trembling. "I'm going to call Navarre now. He can pick up Spotwood and take it from there. Any objections?"

"What about Linda?" she asked. "Do you think she—"

"Had a part in the killing? I don't think so, but it's a chance you've got to take. I've done all I can do for you. I think Linda knows that Spotwood killed Lapham, but maybe she couldn't help it, and after it was

done she decided to protect Spotwood, and to keep secret her marriage to Lapham. That's why she refused
to talk. But now it's police business." I placed my hand
on the phone. "O.K.?"

"Yes," she said, but she was still pale and was gazing about uneasily.

"What's the matter?"

"I—I guess I've got the shakes. That's why I came
in. I was afraid out there in the car. Do you suppose
Arthur is still near—maybe hiding?"

"Killers don't hang around," I told her. "He's
probably back at his gas station wiping windshields."

She leaned against the doorframe. Her gaze fell on
Dr. Otten and flicked away. "I think I see it now—why
Arthur did it. He knew that Linda was seeing Allan,
and he sneaked into Allan's apartment, maybe intend-
ing to kill Allan, because of jealousy. But you surprised
him, and he had to run...." She sighed and went on, "I
felt almost sorry for Allan this evening when I saw him
with that bandage on his forehead. He—he looked so
pale, and so unhappy."

"Getting that old feeling for Allan again?" I asked
as I picked up the phone and held it to my ear.

"Of course not," she said, and she turned quickly
away and walked into the shabby waiting room.
"Hurry," she said. "Please hurry."

I wasn't getting any response from the phone and I
jiggled the cradle bar. Still nothing. No buzz, no answering voice, just dead silence. The phone was dead.
I peered around behind the desk and I saw the wire
from the bell box hanging loosely, with the cut end of
the wire to the phone on the floor.

I mused upon the fact for a second, mentally giving
Arthur Spotwood credit for great foresight. The cut
phone wire meant that he wanted time to get away, far
away, to make a run for it. But I didn't think he'd leave
without Linda, if he could get her out of the house under the noses of the three cops. And then I realized that

he wasn't fool enough to try a stunt like that, not Arthur Spotwood. But was he? Maybe there was another reason for the cut wire.

Slowly I cradled the dead phone and took a deep, long breath. I could see Vivian Prosper standing by the squat oak table in the waiting room. She was gazing at the opposite wall, where the fireplace was, and even in the ugly naked yellow light she looked marvelous. In profile her features were sharp and clean and the tawny hair was the color of ripe wheat. The snug bodice of the lime-green dress hugged her slender waist and caressed the smooth rounded swell of her breasts. She was smoking a cigarette and her cheeks depressed into small hollows as she drew on it.

As I stood gazing at her, it suddenly seemed as if the words she had just spoken were hanging in the room like a neon sign. "I felt almost sorry for Allan this evening when I saw him with that bandage on his forehead." If she had simply said "head" I might have missed it. But she had said "*fore*head." Even so, I was lucky to have remembered. Very, very lucky. And now the events of the last two days crawled across my brain and one by one the things that people did and said fell into a slot.

"Vivian," I said softly.

She looked quickly toward me.

"The phone is dead. Wire cut."

She stared at me, the cigarette poised, the smoke swirling upward into eddying rings around her head. "Arthur cut it, after …?"

I shook my head slowly. "No, not Arthur Spotwood."

"But I don't understand."

"Keeler," I said. "Your sad, poetic ex-husband with the bandage on his goddamned pale forehead, Allan Frederick Keeler. He killed Steve Lapham and Dr. Otten and he tried twice to kill me."

She stared at me blankly.

I fished a cigarette from the crumpled pack in my pocket, and as I struck a match I said, "Get in your car and go to the nearest telephone and call Navarre. I'll stay here." I held the match to my cigarette.

She didn't answer me and it seemed that an ominous quiet had fallen over the dusty office of the late Dr. L. M. Otten. My cigarette fired and I waved out the match and looked up at Vivian Prosper. She was standing rigidly, not looking at me, but away from me at something beyond my vision, something in the vicinity of the fireplace in Dr. Otten's waiting room. Then slowly she backed away from the table and I watched her come toward me, slowly and carefully, step by step, her cigarette held in her hand halfway to her lips. She backed into the office and one high heel struck the limp dead arm of Dr. Otten. She stopped then, still not looking at me, but staring out at something not seen by me. Her lips were parted slightly and her eyes in the slant of profile were wide, and they held, from what I could see of them, a look of fear, of terror, maybe, and I moved quickly away from the desk, not knowing what to expect or what was expected of me.

I'm not much of a quick-draw boy, but my brain signaled my hand and my hand started upward for the gun in my pocket, but far, far too slowly. And then it was too late and I stood frozen, staring into the wicked little black hole that was the muzzle bore of the gun in the hand of Allan Frederick Keeler.

Chapter Seventeen

He had appeared in the doorway without sound and he stood gazing at me and at Vivian with sad, haunted eyes. The gun was a little stubby-barreled .22 revolver. The bandage was still on his forehead, white against the waxy pallor of his thin face, and he was dressed the

same as when I had last seen him in front of my apartment, but now the green-dotted bow tie hung loose
from his open collar and there were red splashes on the
front of his white shirt. A loop of his silky hair drooped
damply over one side of his forehead, reaching almost
to his left eye, and the corners of his thin, sensitive
mouth turned down sadly beneath the blond mustache. He looked more than ever like a despondent
poet.

Vivian Prosper took one slow step backward, and
once again her high heel struck the limp arm of the
dead man. She stood still. "Allan ..." she whispered.

A car went by on the road, and it was a faraway
lonely sound. I found my voice, but when I spoke the
words didn't make sense. I think I said, "What are you
doing here?" or something like that.

"Don't move, either of you," he said in a low dis-
tinct voice. His gaze shifted to me. "I heard you tell
Vivian that I killed Lapham and—him." He indicated
the body of Dr. Otten with the gun. "I can't let either
of you leave here now." He paused and sighed. "I've
botched it. I know I've made mistakes, that I'm just an
amateur, but I'm curious. What made you realize that
I was a murderer? How did you figure it out?"

My cigarette was burning my fingers and I said,
"I'm going to drop my cigarette."

"All right," he said. "Then step on it. You, too,
Vivian."

We dropped our cigarettes to the worn linoleum
and stepped on them. Vivian's made a burned smudge
beside Dr. Otten's thin, lifeless old hand. I felt like a
man in a dream, a bad dream that haunts you when
sleep is over and you are walking in the sunlight. It
seemed suddenly very quiet and I realized that the rain
had stopped. Another car went past the house and it
sounded farther away than the other one. From the
front porch a cricket began to chirp and from somewhere close a night bird cried.

Keeler said quietly, "Please tell me."

I began to talk. It was better than just standing there waiting for him to make up his mind to shoot. "You had me fooled," I said, and my voice sounded all right, "until a few minutes ago, when Vivian made a remark about that bandage on your forehead. I should have caught it in the beginning. You slugged yourself on the head to throw me off the track, to make me think that somebody was after you too, maybe the killer of Lapham. I know now that you faked the head injury, because you told me that you didn't get a look at your attacker, because he struck you from *behind*. And yet the wound was in front, on your forehead.

"I've been dumb as hell. I knew you were a pharmacist, but I figured that as a murder suspect you were too obvious, too pat. But, after all, you are still the only person in this mess who has access to drugs—except Dr. Otten, and he's dead. Morphine for Linda, atropine for me, and—"

"And a scalpel for Lapham, the good doctor, and an ignorant, crude waitress named Blanche," he said.

"Blanche Dorinda Swickert," I said. "So you killed her, too? Because you saw her talking to me, and you followed us to her apartment, fearing that she was going to identify you to me. Did she really know you?"

"Yes," he said. "She really knew me. She used to work in a bar on the other side of town, a place I formerly frequented. She knew my name. I was quite surprised to see her working in the Venice Café when I went there with Linda and Stephen Lapham. But I didn't worry too much about it until I saw you talking to her. When you took her home I knew that your only reason for doing so was to get information from her. So, when you left, I went in and killed her. I had to, you see, to keep her from telling you that I was the other man with Linda. If she had already told you, I didn't want her to be able to testify as a witness. That's why I killed her. It was necessary, don't you see?"

"Yes, I see," I said. "And I'll say this: You did a good job of tailing me. I never spotted you at all."

"Thank you," he said gravely. "I was very careful that you didn't see me."

"A scalpel?" I asked. "A surgeon's scalpel? Is that what you used?"

"Yes, a truly lovely instrument." Deftly he switched the gun to his left hand and from the breast pocket of his brown tweed jacket he drew a slender steel knife, the thin curved blade glinting in the light. The sight and the feel of the naked blade seemed to excite him. The sad look left his eyes and they became cold and flat. His thin lips lost their melancholy droop and I saw the white gleam of his teeth beneath the mustache. It seemed to me that a cold wind swept through the old house.

He hefted the scalpel lovingly and smiled very pleasantly at Vivian and then at me. "The Autopsy Special," he said softly. "The favorite of the world's top pathologists. The Apex Drug Company has exclusive distributing rights in this territory. A little gem of a scalpel. Made of the finest Swedish steel. It's laboratory-tested, and it's quick and quiet, and ever so sharp, and—"

"Allan," Vivian said in a choked voice, "you're mad!"

He gazed at her, still smiling pleasantly. "Of course I'm mad, darling. Certainly I'm mad—about your little sister, Linda! Didn't you know? Why couldn't you have been more like her?" The sad poet was completely gone now; he was gay, friendly, and exhilarated. But there was nothing friendly in his eyes, just that flat coldness, and I knew that if I ever hoped to walk out of this hot, blood-smelling room with Vivian I would have to kill him, if I could. It was a game, a fabulously exciting game for Keeler, but a grim matter of survival for Vivian and me.

I took a short experimental step toward him. Instantly the gun in his hand came up and steadied, and something inside of me twisted and tightened. I stood still.

Keeler laughed, a soft friendly sound. "Please, Mr. Brice. Everything in proper order." He stopped smiling and said seriously, "You know, this may sound odd, but I am enjoying this immensely. Isn't that odd?"

"Why did you kill Lapham?" I asked. "Just simple jealousy? Because he was married to Linda?"

He caressed his mustache with the muzzle of the little revolver and said thoughtfully, "That's a good question, Mr. Brice. No, it wasn't entirely jealousy, although I suppose I was jealous, too. But you see, his marriage to Linda prevented me from marrying her. I love Linda dearly, and, if you don't mind a purely mercenary note, I love the Prosper money, too." He cocked an eyebrow at Vivian. "You spoiled me, darling, and I found it difficult to exist on a pharmacist's salary. After Linda confessed to me that she had inadvertently married Lapham, I went to Lapham and tried to persuade him to quietly divorce her. But he had learned of Linda's inheritance and he just laughed at me. However, other pressure was being exerted upon him, something about a college girl whom he'd got with child, and he finally agreed to discuss a divorce. The three of us—Linda, Lapham, and myself—met at the Venice Café two nights ago. But in his greed Lapham wanted ten thousand dollars to consent to a divorce. Linda didn't have access to that much money, and of course I have been financially embarrassed ever since Vivian was cruel enough to divorce me. I tried to reason with Lapham. I asked him to divorce Linda, let me marry her, and with Linda's inheritance I would pay him. But he was stubborn. He wanted the money in advance." He paused, sighed, and added, "I knew then that I would have to kill him." He smiled at me.

"Don't look so tense, Mr. Brice. And please do not attempt anything foolhardy. Oh, I know that big rugged detectives carry guns. But you can see that I have a gun, too. However, I prefer the Autopsy Special."

Still smiling, but with the queer flat light in his eyes, he moved slowly toward me. Without shifting his gaze, he said to Vivian, "Perhaps you'd better look the other way, darling. There's bound to be a little unpleasantness, even with the Autopsy Special."

I stood like a post and I felt sweat on my ribs. I was scared blue, but still I was filled with a cold rage. A couple of plans moved across my brain and maybe one of them would work, but I had Vivian to think about and anything I did would have to be sudden and final. My fingers ached for the gun in my coat pocket, but he stood six feet away from me, almost point-blank range for his little revolver, and he also held his damned scalpel poised—for the *coup de grâce*, I suppose. I knew I could get to him, but I'd take a bullet, maybe two, on the way, and maybe Vivian would get clear and maybe she wouldn't. I had to be certain of that. I looked at her and I had a feeling of pride. She stood tall and cold and still, her eyes on her one-time husband, and I saw fear in them, certainly, but there was also a deep loathing and a high courage. I was proud as hell of her and I said, "I'm sorry, honey." As soon as I said it I realized with a faint odd embarrassment that it was the first time I'd called her by anything but her name.

She gave me a quick pale smile. "Don't move, Andy," she said. "Don't do anything for me."

Keeler paused in his slow advance. There were tiny globules of sweat on his high pale forehead and at the roots of his yellow hair. "I hope you both understand how it is with me," he said. "I'm in this little drama rather deeply and can't allow either of you to go to the police. I was careful about fingerprints and other things, but, as I said, I'm just an amateur. Perhaps I'll learn as the years go by. But the simple fact, from my viewpoint, is that two more dead bodies won't matter now." He looked at Vivian and for a brief instant the old expression of sadness came to his face. "Please don't look so frightened, darling. I'll be very gentle and quick. First Mr. Brice, and then you. It won't be so bad, really."

He balanced the scalpel lightly in his hand, the blade tilted upward, and he smiled brightly and engagingly at the two of us. "But why am I in such a hurry?" he said. "We have plenty of time. No one knows that we are here and I have cut the telephone wire. Wouldn't you two like to hear how I killed Steve Lapham and Dr. Otten? I'd love to tell you. After all, I'll never have a chance to tell anyone else."

"Except the devil," I said. "He'll enjoy it."

"How droll," he said, and for an instant there was a flame in his eyes and I thought he was going to shoot. But the flame died, leaving again the queer flat coldness, and he said in a friendly conversational tone, "Let me see if I can remember the rather interesting events leading to our meeting here. Where was I? Oh, yes. After my fruitless conversation with the stubborn and greedy college boy, the three of us left the Venice Café and went to the parking lot in the rear where Linda had left her car. It was late and the lot was deserted. Lapham was quite drunk and Linda and I were still attempting to persuade him to agree to the divorce. He became enraged and he struck me. Then he turned on Linda and struck her. She fell, hitting her head on the rear bumper of her car. In his rage Lapham kicked her, and that is when I intervened. In anticipation of trouble, I had taken a scalpel from the store, and I also had the revolver. But the scalpel is silent and I took it from my pocket. Lapham rushed at me madly and I slipped the blade into his chest. He died almost instantly. It was easy, easier than I'd ever dreamed. Did you ever kill a man, Mr. Brice?"

"No," I said, and I added, "Not yet."

"Too bad you can't try it sometime," he said. "You'd enjoy it. It's so easy and it gives one a tremendous feeling of power." He sighed. "But there I was, with a dead man at my feet, and Linda unconscious from striking her head. Well, I thought fast, and I put Lapham's body in the rear of Linda's car and removed all possible identification. Then I picked up Linda, placed her on the front seat, and drove across town to the store where I work. I entered the rear door with my key, got morphine and a hypo needle from stock, and returned to the car.... Am I boring you?"

"Not at all," I said. "It's extremely interesting. Please continue."

He gave me his friendly smile. "And, besides, the longer I talk, the longer you'll live. I suppose you are considering that?"

"Yes," I said.

Vivian made some kind of sound. Not a gasp, just a small sound, not a sigh or a cry. It sounded something like the mewing of a kitten. I glanced at her, but she still stood tall and stiff and erect, her eyes on Keeler. It seemed to me that she'd been standing in that attitude for hours. How long had this been going on? How long would it continue to go on? I felt as though something within me was about to snap with a sharp audible crack.

"I enjoy talking about it," Keeler said, "if you still care to listen."

"Go on," I heard my voice say.

"Thank you," he said courteously. "I am pleased that you enjoy my little story.... Well, I was very fortunate. Linda did not regain consciousness until after we arrived back at the Venice Café. Then I gave her an injection of morphine so that she would remain quiet. I went into the Café and sat at the bar. Now I must digress a moment. You see, Linda had told me that a stupid gasoline-station oaf named Arthur Spotwood

wanted to marry her. And so when an elderly gentleman at the bar—we were practically the last patrons in
the place—introduced himself to me as a Dr. Otten, I
told him that my name was Arthur Spotwood. It
amused me, and you must also understand that I
hadn't quite decided what to do with Lapham's body.
Naturally, I wished to protect myself as much as possible. If there was a chance of connecting Spotwood
with Lapham's death, so much the better. Besides, Dr.
Otten told me that he had observed me in the Café earlier in the evening, and he asked me what had become
of the girl and the other man. I told him that I had
taken them home and came back for a nightcap. Don't
you think that was clever of me?"

"Very," I said.

"After establishing my identity with Dr. Otten," he
went on, "I left the Café and drove around trying to
decide what to do with Lapham's body. Linda came
partially out of the morphine and I gave her another
injection." He paused and once more the sadness returned to his eyes. "I hated to do it—it was really a
dangerous dose on top of the first one—but I had no
choice. I couldn't risk having Linda make a fuss and
attract attention—not with a dead man in the car. So I
drove around some more. I enjoyed it greatly, driving
in the night with the girl I loved beside me and a man
I hated in the rear. Once I stopped in the country beneath a tall pine tree and I wanted to make love to
Linda, but she didn't respond. That angered me and
for a mad moment I wanted to kill her, too. It was very
strange and—beautiful. Can you understand that?"

"Shoot," I said in a choked voice. "Shoot, you sonofabitch. Squeeze that trigger and swing that fancy
knife and let's see what happens. Come on, you bastard." My muscles tensed to leap for him.

Vivian's voice stopped me. "No, Andy! No!"

I stood trembling. I could feel the sweat on my face.

Keeler laughed softly. "Oh, this is really fun! Mr. Brice, you look so—so ludicrous. Don't you want to hear the rest?"

I couldn't answer him. I couldn't speak.

Vivian said in a quiet soothing voice, "Yes. Allan. Please continue."

He gave her a mock bow. "Thank you, darling. You are as gracious as always, but I'm afraid that Mr. Brice is letting his emotions get the better of him." He looked at me and said seriously, "Death isn't so terrible. Why are you so afraid to die? When I sat beneath the pine tree with Linda in my arms, death seemed like a sweet friend, to Linda and to me. I caressed her throat with my fingers and it would have been so easy to quench out her life, and mine, too, with the scalpel. I intended to do it, and I loved thinking about it, but the dawn came so quickly, and then the sun, and cars began to go past on the road. I became a little confused then, and somewhat frightened, and I knew that it was too late to do anything about Lapham's body. So I drove to a roadside restaurant, brought black coffee out to Linda, and forced it down her. When she was partially revived I drove her home, headed the car into the drive, turned off the motor, and jumped out. The car coasted down the drive and stopped."

He paused and smiled at me. "Can you guess what I did then, Mr. Brice?"

The cricket out by the porch had stopped chirping, but the night bird still cried forlornly. A car hadn't gone past in a long time and I wondered what time of the morning it was. Vivian Prosper still stood erect, and once more I had the feeling of pride in her, of admiration. She had courage and I hoped she wouldn't crack. Very soon now we would have to face the hell in Keeler's heart and mind, and I told myself that when I made a move, as I must do sooner or later, it would be a move to protect her as much as possible. I could jump for him now, and there was a good chance that I

would get to him, even with the bullets in me, but I
had to be sure he didn't live. If I died, he must die, and
Vivian would be left—if I played it right.

It was not a question of heroics, but a question of
settling for the best possible bargain. But a bleakness
filled me when I thought of all the things in life I liked:
the first cigarette after the first cup of coffee in the
morning, the feel of a hot shower and clean clothes,
the music I still wanted to hear, the books I still wanted
to read, the women I'd loved and the women who
might come later, rain on a summer night, the first
frosty morning in October, a drink before dinner, the
memory of my father and mother and the farm in
Ohio, my brother and my sister and my sister's kids,
blue water and warm sand on a sunny beach, cold beer
in locker rooms after eighteen holes of golf—all the
things I loved that made up my sometimes lonely but
always satisfying life. It was maybe a selfish, unim-
portant life, but it was mine, and I wanted to keep it.
If I could.

I said to Keeler, "I can guess what you did then, but
I'd rather hear you tell it." I watched for a crack in his
vigilance, but none came. In spite of his easy, mocking
manner, he never relaxed for an instant.

"Thank you," he said. He glanced at Vivian.
"Would you like me to continue?"

"Allan," she said, "listen ..."

He made an impatient gesture. "Don't plead with
me. It will get you nothing. Don't you see my position?"

"Yes, Allan, I see, but—"

"Stop, damn you!" he shouted, and for an instant
the flame appeared in his eyes. Then he took a deep
shuddering breath. "I'm sorry, darling. Naturally you
don't want to die. Unfortunately, neither do I." He
lifted his shoulders. "You see? Survival of the fittest,
and all that. After all, we're living in a jungle, really,

and these things happen every day." He looked at me. "Don't they, Mr. Brice?"

"Every day," I said.

I had just about made up my mind to do it, to do something. But still I waited, watching him, and I wondered if I could hold out to the precise moment, if there was going to be a precise moment, if there was ever going to be anything for me in this world but bullets in my chest or my stomach or wherever Keeler chose to send them. I wanted to shout wildly and leap for him, to get it over with, to wind it up in bullets and the scalpel and hope that Vivian would get away in the confusion of the final messy struggle. But I waited, I didn't know for what. I was still alive, and so was Vivian, and every minute now was a shining dividend.

Maybe Keeler sensed what was in my mind, or perhaps he saw it in my eyes. He said, "Don't get impatient, Mr. Brice. I'll make it as brief as I can. You have a right to know, and I really want to tell you. After Linda's car stopped in the drive, I waited across the street. I saw you and Vivian come out of the house in response to the blowing of the horn, and I saw you carry Linda inside. I waited some more. Then Arthur Spotwood came and left, and later I saw the police arrive. I left then, but not before I'd taken down the license number of your car. A phone call to the county recorder of motor vehicles gave me your name and occupation. I became a little suspicious then, but I wasn't worried about Linda's talking too much or involving me. She didn't want anyone to know about her marriage to Lapham, or her—ah—friendship with me. And besides, she had been unconscious when I killed Lapham. So I followed you from that time until now. Does that explain a number of things?"

"Yes," I said. "It does. You guessed that I was picking up your trail at the Venice Café, and you decided to eliminate me. So you faked a phone call from one of the booths in the Café, and while I was gone from my

194   ROBERT MARTIN

table you slipped a hefty dose of atropine into my drink. By the way, how did you happen to have the drug with you?"

"A reasonable question," he said seriously, "and I am pleased to explain. I had a supply in my car. I was supposed to deliver it to another drugstore in the city. I would have preferred a combination of prussic acid and cyanide of potassium, or maybe arsenic and veronal, but I did the best I could under the circumstances. Atropine in sufficient quantity is very—effective. And if that meddling old fool"—he indicated the body of Dr. Otten—"hadn't been so handy, the atropine would have been just dandy. That's a poem, isn't it? Handy and dandy? You see, atropine is the most important of the alkaloids in *Atropa belladonna*, or deadly nightshade. Nightshade. I like that word. It has an attractively eerie sound, don't you think?" His voice was still steady and pleasant, but his eyes held now a new expression. The coldness was gone and there was excitement and anticipation in them, and I knew that he was wearing it too thin, that he had come close to the outer edge of his particular brand of psychopathic pleasurable torture, and now he wanted to get on with it, to the climax, the real ecstasy.

I made quick words. "Dr. Otten saved my life. You hung around and you knew that your scheme to poison me had failed. So you continued to tail me, to see what I would do next. When I went to your apartment, you decided to stage a little act to gain sympathy for yourself and to confuse things a little. You entered your apartment ahead of me by a rear door, hit yourself on the head, and waited for me to find you."

He nodded agreeably. "Quite correct, and very clever of you. I slipped up on that. But, as I said, I'm just an amateur. I should have struck myself on the *back* of the head, so that it would have jibed with my story." He sighed and gave me an apologetic look. "But I couldn't think of everything. I'd been through a rather trying night and morning, and perhaps I wasn't thinking too clearly. But the bump I gave myself with a hammer hurt quite severely, nevertheless.... You know, listening to you tell it is almost as much fun as telling it myself."

"Thanks," I said, and I thought wildly, The more words, the longer time Vivian and I will have. "I'll tell you some more. This afternoon you saw me leave the Venice Café with the waitress and go to her apartment. As you said, you were worried about what she might tell me, or had already told me. So after I left you went up to her apartment and killed her, just to make certain that she wouldn't testify against you. You had already killed once, and it didn't matter too much to you. You followed me to Midstate University and to the house where Dorothy Toynbee lives, and you saw me talking to Navarre. Then you really began to sweat. So you stuck to me. After Vivian and I had dinner at the Venice Café you hurried back to my place so that you would he waiting for us. Then you gave me a fake story about receiving a threatening telephone call, lied again about not seeing Linda, and professed your undying love for Vivian—all calculated to throw me off the scent. It worked, too, I'm sorry to say.

"But still you hung around. When Vivian and I headed for Dr. Otten's house, you followed and got scared all over again. That's what a guilty conscience does to a person. You were afraid that Dr. Otten, in spite of your build-up in representing yourself to him as Arthur Spotwood, perhaps knew your real identity, or had described you to me. So you passed us on the road, hurried ahead, and stabbed the doctor just before we arrived, to keep him from talking. But still you hung around, like a damned vulture. Why, for God's sake?"

"You know," he said, and his voice was ragged now, "this amuses me less and less. I seem to be bored with the whole thing. But I want you to know this: I had plenty of time to get away before you arrived. But I wanted to get your reaction to my—ah—handiwork. So I hid in the darkness of the other room and listened. I am very glad that I did. I heard you tell Vivian that the doctor had named Spotwood as his murderer, which pleased me very much. And then you killed my joy by pronouncing sentence on me. I knew then what I had to do—and the time for doing it is past."

Still stalling for a little more time, I said, "I should have gone gunning for you right after I knew that Linda had been doped with morphine, but I had no reason to—then. I didn't even tumble when Dr. Otten told me about the atropine, although I knew you were a pharmacist. But it adds up to three killings, and—"

"Correction," Keeler broke in softly. "*Five* killings. I'm not finished yet. Aren't you forgetting Vivian and yourself?"

I didn't answer him. I couldn't think of anything more to say. The talking time was gone. I took a slow step forward. To hell with him. Let him shoot. I was all through standing still for him. The step placed me at the head of the leather-covered table, with the length of the table between us. In his right fist he held the scalpel, the thin bright blade tilted upward. He crouched a little, like an animal about to spring, and his eyes were bright and alert and cunning and filled with what looked to me like an ecstasy of anticipation.

"Thank you for moving," he murmured. Even his voice had changed. It was low and thick, heavy with almost sexual excitement. "Dr. Otten also sought the table for protection, and that is where I made the incision. On the table. See the bright red blood?"

He kept creeping forward and I wondered if now was the time to go for my gun. But he was watching me narrowly, his revolver pointed straight at my chest. Wait, wait, I told myself. I shot a quick glance at Vivian. She was still standing tall and straight, her gaze on

Keeler, her face a pale red-lipped mask. I faced Keeler once more.

"I'm sure you have a gun," he muttered thickly. "Why don't you use it?"

He really wanted me to make the attempt. It would add to his pleasure. Between his ready gun and his damned scalpel he knew I wouldn't have a chance. I knew it too, but it was better than standing still and waiting for the bullets to hit me. He laughed deep in his throat, showing his white teeth.

"Please," he coaxed. "Come on, be a sport. Let's have fun."

He stopped his slow crouching movement forward and for a long second we eyed each other like a snake and a mouse. I was the mouse. Then his lips closed over his teeth and his eyes, half hooded by the lids, glinted liquidly. My stomach seemed to turn over and I felt sick. The gun in his hand bore on me steadily and the scalpel was poised, bright and shining and razor-sharp. I saw his finger curl lovingly over the trigger of the gun and I could hear his sudden fast breathing, like an excited lover coming to his sweetheart's bed.

Wildly I gauged the distance to him and I tensed myself for a lunge that I hoped would take me to him before his bullets finished their job. A booming voice in my brain screamed, *Now!*

Something horrible erupted in the little room. A shrill, terror-ridden sound, starting on a low hoarse note, a guttural animal sound, and climbing fast to a graveyard wail. It wasn't human and it made my flesh crawl and writhe and my ears wanted to reject it. And yet I knew that it was human—a human voice screaming beyond mortal limits.

And then, abruptly, in the middle of it, I knew what it was. Vivian Prosper was uttering the granddaddy of all the nightmare screams in the world.

Keeler shot a quick glance at her. He had to. Nobody could ignore that ear-splitting sound. Instantly he recovered and swung back toward me, but I was moving at last and I pushed the wheeled leather table forward with all my strength. The edge smashed into his stomach and he gasped sharply and jackknifed over it. I jumped clear and jerked my .32 loose from my pocket.

Keeler writhed like a snake on the table. His arms were doubled beneath him and his feet thumped the floor in a wild tattoo. Then he rolled toward me, over the table, and the light glinted on the gun in his hand. I squeezed the trigger of the .32, aiming for his head, where it would do the most good, but he was a fast-moving target, and as the gun bucked in my hand and the room rocked with the muzzle blast I knew that I had missed. I jumped out of the path of his tumbling body and steadied my gun for a more careful shot. He landed on his back across the legs of Dr. Otten and carefully I aimed the .32 at his left eye.

But he didn't move and my finger relaxed on the trigger. Then I saw the polished steel handle of the scalpel protruding from the left side of his chest and the blood slowly staining the front of his white shirt, mingling with the darker stain of Dr. Otten's blood already there. I stared dumbly; and then I realized that when he had doubled over the table he had impaled himself on the uptilted blade of the scalpel in his hand.

He took maybe three or four deep gulps of air before he died. Blood ran from his mouth and over his chin and stained his silky yellow mustache before it finally strangled him. His eyes rolled upward and his back arched and for an instant I thought he was screaming silently. And then he was quiet. He didn't look like a poet any more. He just looked very dead.

I turned slowly to look at Vivian Prosper. The back of one hand was pressed against her teeth and the scream was dying in her wide eyes.

"You all right?" I asked her. My voice sounded loud and queer in the quiet room.

She lowered her hand and looked at it. There was blood on it from her teeth. "Y-yes," she said in a faint voice.

"Thanks for that scream," I said.

She tried to smile, but she couldn't quite make it. It was just a stiff movement of her lips. "I—I never scream," she said. "I told you that. It—it's a sign of weakness. But I thought it would be a good time to be weak." She placed a hand to her throat. "I think my vocal cords are severed."

She fumbled a cigarette from a pocket of the lime-green skirt and she tried to light it, but her hands were shaking too much. I moved over to her and struck a match, but my hands were shaking too and her cigarette didn't get lit. We gazed at each other over the trembling flame, and there in that room with two dead men at our feet, we began to laugh like a couple of crazy people.

THE END

Robert Lee Martin was born on October 16, 1908, in Chula, Virginia, to Joseph and Harriet (Repasz) Martin. He graduated from Columbian High School of Tiffin, Ohio in 1927. Martin was a bank teller for the First National Bank of Tiffin from 1928 until 1934, then became a stock clerk at the Sterling Grinding Wheel Company in Tiffin in 1934. Martin was their stock department manager from 1936 to 1941, and an assistant in the personnel department from 1941 to 1945. He married Alverta Mae Smith in 1942, and they had two daughters and a son. Martin became the assistant personnel manager from 1945 to 1950 and then the personnel manager. He wrote 23 detective novels between 1951 and 1964, including the Jim Bennett series under his own name, and various other mysteries as by "Lee Roberts." He died in Tiffin on February 1, 1976.

Robert Lee Martin Bibliography
(1908-1976)

NOVELS

Jim Bennett series:
Dark Dream (Dodd Mead, 1951; Pocket, 1952).
Sleep, My Love (Dodd Mead, 1953; Dell, 1953)
Tears for the Bride (Dodd Mead, 1954; Bantam, 1955)
The Widow and the Web (Dodd Mead, 1954; Bantam, 1955)
The Echoing Shore (Dodd Mead, 1955; Bantam, 1957, as The Tough Die Hard)
Just a Corpse at Twilight (Dodd Mead, 1955)
Catch a Killer (Dodd Mead, 1956; abridged in *Mercury Mystery Book Magazine*)
Hand-Picked for Murder (Dodd Mead, 1957)
Killer Among Us (Dodd Mead, 1958; Detective Book Club, 1959)
A Key to the Morgue (Dodd Mead, 1959; Detective Book Club, 1959; Ace, 1960)
To Have and To Kill (Dodd Mead, 1960; Ace, 1961, abridged)
She, Me and Murder (Hale UK, 1962; Curtis, 1971)
A Coffin for Two (Hale UK, 1962; Curtis, 1972)
Bargain for Death (Hale UK, 1964, Curtis, 1972)

As by Lee Roberts

Little Sister (Gold Medal, 1952)
The Pale Door (Dodd Mead, 1955; Detective Book Club, 1955; Bantam, 1956)
Judas Journey (Dodd Mead, 1956; Popular Library, 1957)
The Case of the Missing Lovers (Dodd Mead, 1957)

Dr. Clinton Shannon series:

Once a Widow (Dodd Mead, 1957; Detective Book
Club, 1957; Dell, 1959)
If the Shoe Fits (Dodd Mead, 1959; Crest, 1960)
Death of a Ladies' Man (Gold Medal, 1960)
Suspicion (Hale UK, 1964; Curtis, 1971)

Black Gat Books

Black Gat Books is a new line of mass market paperbacks introduced in 2015 by Stark House Press. New titles appear every three months, featuring the best in crime fiction reprints. Each book is size to 4.25" x 7", just like they used to be, and priced at $9.99. Collect them all.

Stark House Press
1315 H Street, Eureka, CA 95501 707-498-3135 griffinskye3@sbcglobal.net www.starkhousepress.com Available from your local bookstore or direct from the publisher.

Made in the USA
Monee, IL
04 December 2020